In Our
Bones

In Our Bones

Pernell Plath Meier

Copyright © 2020 Pernell Plath Meier.

Cover Design by Suzanne Johnson

Willow River Press
Between the Lines Publishing
410 Caribou Trail
Lutsen, MN 55612
btwnthelines.com

First Published: 2020

Willow River Press is an imprint of Between the Lines Publishing.
The Willow River Press name and logo are trademarks of Between the Lines Publishing.

The publisher is not responsible for websites (or their content) that are not owned by the publisher.

ISBN: 978-1-950502-30-1 (paperback)
Printed in the United States

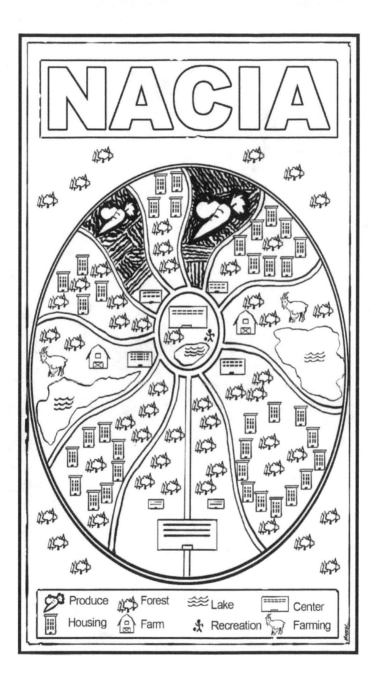

NACIA

🥕 Produce	🌲 Forest	〰️ Lake	▭ Center
🏠 Housing	🏠 Farm	🏃 Recreation	🐐 Farming

The TVs Went Blank

Lauren's phone buzzed, bringing reality crashing into her sleep. She lay motionless for a moment, gathering consciousness, as her head throbbed, and dryness puckered her mouth. She groped the nightstand for the device without opening her eyes, already knowing by the ringtone who was calling and why. She put the phone to her ear.

"Hey," she croaked. "Okay... Sure."

She tossed the phone on the bed next to her and curled up back into a restless sleep. When the phone pinged another notification, she knew she needed to get up and tried to start waking. She opened one eye, then the next as she yawned and stretched. She reached around and found the phone again to check the time. Only three hours.

The air in the house was cool as she threw back her fuzzy blankets and resisted their Siren's song to crawl back in.

"Fucking Vivian," she muttered, dragging herself to the bathroom.

Blinding warm sunshine blasted the open door as she stepped inside. A huge window dominated the royal purple bathroom with crystal suncatchers filling the glass, splitting the light into its constituent parts and sending rainbows dancing across the walls. This room was Lauren's favorite. She'd never had the money to fix up her whole house the way she'd wanted, but her dad had found the claw foot tub and pedestal sink at an auction and restored them to their former glory. Before he got sick, Dale did things like that for her all the time. He was an attentive father to both Lauren and her sister, Rachel. Though it seemed there was always a little something extra for her, as if he was trying to make up for some wrong he thought he'd committed. Lauren never could tell him why things really changed between them.

Lauren climbed into the shower and the hot steam combined with the tingle of her homemade peppermint cleanser to bring some life back to her. As she brushed her hair and put on a thin row of eyeliner, she avoided gazing into her own eyes, since seeing dejection staring back was too much most days. She threw on a pair of black leggings and plain t-shirt as she wandered into the kitchen, connecting her phone to the Bluetooth speaker and filling the room with her tunes. She poured a bowl of cereal and plopped down at the table, still shaky from her drinking binge the night before - a binge which had been prompted by a single word in the form of a text message. Hey. It ripped open the scab that had finally begun to heal since her boyfriend started ghosting her the month before. Lauren had texted and called over and again, but nothing but a string of unread messages was left to show for their year-long relationship. She was reeling from the suddenness of the separation, since without someone by her side, she felt incomplete. She could end her torture with him now and flick her finger across Delete, but that would mean facing a different torment -single again. More frightening still was her need to be needed. She wanted to be strong and was terrified of anyone seeing she wasn't. Unfortunately, the endless parade of loser boyfriends was a dead giveaway, and anyone who took the time to know her could see the shattered girl beneath her vivid green eyes.

Lauren looked into her soggy bowl of cereal, thankful to be at the end as her stomach was still a clenched knot. She forced herself to take a few more bites, as she knew her shift at the bar would be intense, and she'd need the energy. Work was fast approaching, and she didn't want to go. She didn't need the job the way others did, including dumbass Vivian. With jobs fewer and farther between, people were making ends meet haphazardly. The economy had continued to erode after the pandemic and sent America even more swiftly down the spiral of dysfunction. Storms, fires, record heat waves and arctic blasts dominated the country and compounded the misery. The federal government was unwilling and incapable of handling any of it.

Even before the frog that was America finally boiled in the pot, Lauren had created for herself an oasis in anticipation of the crisis. On her hobby farm she had shelves stocked with neat rows of home-canned vegetables, whirling turbines pumping fresh water, and gallons of sweet wine, hoppy beer, and corn liquor.

Outwardly, Lauren's life was immaculate, but internally she was a hot mess. She'd arrived at adulthood feeling like an imposter to the status. Other than her house, she had no other visible signals that she'd arrived. In her circle, children and marriage provided the keys to the kingdom of adulthood. Lauren wanted a husband; she knew that for sure. But her lack of interest in motherhood would remain on the fringes of her consciousness as an unthought known for decades to come. The frigid judgment she was already feeling from her friends for not yet having her own was challenging enough, but to not want children at all put Lauren in a category of her own. She tucked away the unsettling thought into a tidy drawer inside the halls of her mind where she kept the truths she most feared. Lauren had stuffed up so much feeling that she could come across as having none. Underneath that icy exterior she was as soft as melted butter, though. She'd never learned how to care while still protecting her heart, fearing that she'd be sucked into an emotional abyss. Lauren built a wall between her heart and mind that was so high and wide she no longer knew how to scale it.

As she readied for her shift, she nursed resentment toward Vivian for calling in yet again. She also nursed her woozy self. Lauren was raised to think of work as both a duty and necessity, as farm life typically meant. Being sick was only an excuse to stay in bed if absolutely necessary, and Lauren's drunken dehydration didn't count in her book. Besides, she liked her manager and appreciated the extra cash in her pocket. As she stood up from the dark wooden chair, she felt her head spin. She muttered, "I shouldn't have finished off the bottle, I guess. It's always that last drink that does it. Or last two. Maybe three…" She scoffed at herself.

She fished a cigarette from her pack and lit a smoke as she considered calling her mother. It was a daily ritual. She didn't actually want to speak with her, since Ann always made her anxious. But Lauren wanted to find out how her father was doing, and Ann was the gatekeeper of the phone. At least Ann would stick to the present situation with her father's health. Dale would go on long political rants nearly every time she spoke with him. Before he was sick, he would never have carried on with her like that, since he knew that this was her least favorite subject. He'd been diagnosed with non-

Hodgkin's lymphoma; the lawyers said it was from the herbicides he used as a farmer. His cancer results came back not long before the COVID-19 pandemic hit. He and everyone in their immediate family survived, unlike the hundreds of thousands of Americans who didn't. Dale claimed that his family made it because of his menagerie of antiviral and medical plants he cultivated and bottled. He fancied himself an amateur herbalist, and this love of plants was one of the only ways Lauren connected to anyone in her family. The smoke from her cigarette floated around the yellow kitchen as she put off calling a few more minutes.

Lauren Hansberry's family life had not always been strained. She felt loved growing up, and was even close with Rachel, her older sister, despite their twenty-year age gap. When Lauren was little, Rachel was warm and affectionate in a way that their mother Ann never was. Lauren used to beg her to stay when she'd be getting ready to leave after a visit from college or her settled life as a librarian in Des Moines. As a child, Rachel's departure would leave a lonely pall over Lauren. Their father worked long hours and being with Ann was often worse than being alone.

As Lauren matured, she was never able to emerge from Rachel's shadow. Of the two sisters, Rachel was the good one, the successful one. While Lauren's sister traveled abroad and collected university degrees, Lauren never found her groove. She'd gone to community college straight out of high school, but she didn't know what she wanted to do and couldn't afford tuition anyway. She dropped out after two semesters. She'd never been out of the Midwest and had no interest in a career in the traditional sense. She wanted something more from life but didn't know what that something else was exactly. Lauren often felt like a failure in her parent's eyes, though she knew they would never have said that aloud. Regardless, she was a failure in her own eyes, and that was what mattered.

Though Lauren was proud of some things about herself, primarily her homesteading skills. Lauren's folks had given her a tiny plot of land off a section of their farm and helped her build a house. Dale insisted that the home she built be able to resist just about any deluge that came their way, since he'd been seeing climate change getting worse for decades atop his tractor. Lauren reluctantly agreed to build that way because she wasn't blind. She'd been seeing the erratic weather herself as gardening was becoming more of a challenge. Her problem was that she couldn't quite believe all her father's talk about a warming planet being so incredibly serious and caused by people alone. Her friends said that it was volcanoes and that the climate had changed many times throughout history already. The libs were being hysterical, they said, and to Lauren that was a more convenient concept to hold in her mind. She had enough on her emotional plate as it was, let alone grappling with the complexities of the world.

Lauren crushed her cigarette in the ashtray and braced herself as the phone rang. Ann answered, "Hello."

"Hey Mom. How's Dad this morning?"

"Well, it would be nice if you asked about me once in a while, too."

"I'm sorry. How are you?"

"It doesn't matter, your father is the one who's sick."

Lauren rolled her eyes. Why the hell did she just tell me to ask how she was, then? She steadied the irritation in her voice. "Yes, I know that. How is he this morning?"

Lauren heard her father in the background. "Is that Laur? Let me talk to her."

Ann blathered over him. "He's been cranky as ever. But he says his pain isn't too bad. I don't know if he's pooped yet today, though."

"That's okay, Mom. I don't really need to know…"

Lauren heard a mild struggle over the phone and then her father come on. She groaned quietly. Dale had changed from a genial man to a vinegary one as his illness wore on. As a young man he was especially involved with the Prairie Populist political movement that swept across the rural Midwest and remained constructively active. He grew bitter, though, as he saw the prairie turn to fascist populism in his sunset years. As Dale understood it, farmers moved away from their roots and from common sense. Dale had been a man of newspapers over lunch and public radio while he worked his crops, so when he retired he had little to do other than roll in and out of each day in a sea of current events. Lauren imagined him as a balloon of information that would pop in an awkward and frantic rush whenever he'd speak to anyone.

Dale huffed after he secured the phone from Ann. "Your mother doesn't need to be telling you personal stuff like that about me. That's ridiculous. But I need to talk to you. I want you to stay home today. I'm really worried about the election after how bad things have gotten. They say the President is moving his police around, and he's got those bikers and so-called patriots out there scaring everyone and stirring up trouble. It's even worse than the last election…"

Lauren tried to be patient. "Dad, I'm sure that's upsetting, but I was calling to hear about you."

Dale ignored his daughter's pleas. "Someday they'll be coming for your sister. I'm too old, you know… But Rachel's been out protesting, and they monitor all that on the social media and everything now. In the end, no one is safe when a dictator can do whatever he wants. These fellas talk a big talk about defending the Constitution, but they're just trying to save their own darned selves if you ask me. They're pretending like they're protecting God and family, but that's a bunch of bull. They're just about hating everyone who's even a little different, or they're just greedy, or looking for revenge. Whatever it is they want; they're never going to give up power... When I'm gone, you have to keep your mom and sister safe. You're stronger than you know, Laur."

Lauren pulled the phone away from her ear for most of the rant and the next few minutes that followed. She learned to insert enough okays and uh-huhs that Dale didn't notice her lack of engagement. Lauren knew her dad was smart and all, but he could still come across as part of the lunatic fringe. Lauren felt like that description could apply to most everyone she knew anymore. Whether they were ranting about the President or ranting because no one properly appreciated the President, it was all the same to her.

Lauren ended the conversation with her usual tenderness. "Okay, Dad. Thanks for letting me know about all that. I'll be careful. I'll stop by tomorrow."

She was relieved to hang up and lit another cancer stick. She blew out the smoke as she hurried to put on her muck boots and tend the hens and goats.

It was sultry for November. By the time Lauren left for work, sunlight had warmed the inside of her Jeep. She flipped on the radio as she sped off down the gravel road, kicking up dust behind her. For Sale signs punctuated the landscape as so many of their neighbors were losing or had lost their farms. Endless trade wars with China and other countries were hollowing out her rural neighborhood. Lauren's thoughts were wandering between her father and her boyfriend as she drove.

The newscast came on: "...three F2 tornadoes touched down in Kansas and Missouri yesterday, killing four. Authorities have called for blood donations..."

Lauren whispered, "Those poor people," and changed the radio station.

The parking lot of the bland strip mall was packed as she pulled into the last remaining spot. She was already five minutes late, as usual. She grabbed her apron and rushed inside. The dimly lit bar bustled; she'd never seen the place so full. As Lauren was clocking in, her manager walked by and gave her an exasperated look.

"At least I showed up!" Lauren shouted as she secured her white blonde hair in a ponytail.

Lauren's manager, always fretting about business, was concerned that national unrest would keep customers away. His drink specials were hot enough to draw out a community still hungry for social interactions after the long isolation of COVID. It helped that their small city had been largely spared the worst of the troubles ravaging the country. Noise from the lunch swarm was deafening as Lauren jumped into the fray and began taking orders from impatient customers. She assembled an enormous tray of drinks and glided across the scuffed linoleum floor like a dancer with a mission. An unknown hand reached out and pinched her ass. She barely flinched, since she'd long since absorbed the notion that she had little autonomy over her body. Taking and delivering orders as fast as she could, the televisions blared with discussions of the day's events.

"Seeing these long lines at the polls across the country, pundits are saying that if voter turn-out were this high two years ago, there was no way the President would have been able to stay in office."

A jovially cantankerous table of the President's most ardent supporters dominated the back corner. Those who ecstatically supported him welcomed the buzz-saw he had taken to common decency. They had been looking for their strong-shouldered leader for some time, and in the President they found a man who embodied alpha masculinity and would happily throw them all the cultural red meat they could swallow. Some segments of the President's supporters also saw him as anointed by God himself to deliver the country from Damnation. Others saw the President as the one who would usher in the End Times and recreate Heaven on Earth. Leaders of the President's political party generally cared little for these droll particularities. Their ambition had been to find an idiot with a pen to sign tax cuts for themselves and their well-heeled acquaintances and reshape the court system in their favor. The marriage of convenience between the President and the ruling Party worked well for all until the mad king they unleashed turned on them, too. The President could not be constrained.

After the President's controversial and highly contested re-election in 2020, his frothing supporters were emboldened. At the bar that night, they were making their opinions clear to anyone within earshot. The President's claim to victory was suspect and highly contested. He'd appointed one of his cronies to run the Postal Service, thus ensuring the flood of mail-in ballots spurred by the virus wouldn't arrive on time to be counted. The President also put out marching orders to his Party and supporters across the land – suppress the vote through any means available. Close any polling place possible in poor and non-white communities and make voting harder. The President and his boot-licking Attorney General sent their private military force to harass voters at polling places and encouraged his minions to join in the fracas. The President's favorite foreign dictators assisted with an all-out campaign of disruption, and the fate of the country was fractured. When the President pulled ahead in early in-person vote counts on election night, he said that the Opposition Party was trying to steal the election, and no other votes should be counted. His hand-picked Supreme Court backed him, and the military stayed silent. Protests lasted months but were eventually crushed in all but the most tenacious quarters. The actual civil war had started years before most Americans were paying attention, though, as attacks had been increasing across the country.

Americans were collectively exhausted with the circus the President created to distract from a failing country. They dreamed of ushering in change during the midterm election. Most of the crowd at Silver Lake Bar and Grill was enthusiastically hopeful as they nibbled their food and sipped their drinks while proudly wearing, I voted stickers. The goal was to flip enough seats in both big and small races across the country to begin to right the moral arc of history. Another rush of customers came flooding in when the sky had long darkened and the televisions began reporting election results. Each time an Opposition Party victory was announced, the place would erupt in cheers. Lauren heard a table start to sing the song, Hey, Hey, Goodbye. The President's people grumbled. Lauren was passing out food orders at one table when she heard a tipsy young woman call out, "We're taking our country back from these goddamned Nazis! I told you, Harper."

As if perfectly timed to dash the woman's hopes, in that second a piercing noise began emanating from the TVs. Lauren lurched toward the bar for the remote to turn it down. Before she could get there, the screens fell dark and quiet. Her leg vibrated from a text. She heard notifications throughout the place as everyone grasped their phones. Lauren slid hers from her pocket and read:

Urgent Alert: Department of Homeland Security. A state of emergency has been issued effective immediately. You will receive a follow up message from your local authorities for further direction.

She remembered her father's warning that morning and looked around the room as people cried and shouted. She glanced over her shoulder at the Party supporters who were victoriously praising the move. "If we've got to have a dictator, I'd rather it be ours." Lauren felt the illness from the morning creep back in as her gut gurgled. She felt faint.

Just as suddenly as the TVs went dark, they all came back on again showing the President and his daughter on the settee in the Oval Office. The President sat slumped with a glazed expression as his daughter observed him with adoration. The President's jaw was taught and his dentures loose, adding to the garble as he read the teleprompter.

"Good evening to all loyal Americans. I've received intelligence of tremendous fraud..." He looked about, haggard and worn. His daughter whispered into his ear with a mouth gleaming with bright lipstick and the whitest teeth money could buy. Her father focused.

"This is voter fraud that we're dealing with. They're trying to overthrow the will of the people, and my administration won't stand for that. We will not let you, the forgotten ones, be forgotten anymore. I stand by your side, defending our country." The President's supporters stood and yelped at this line.

The President's remarks strayed from those prepared for him, "We're rooting out our enemies. Your enemies! When they attack me, your great President, they are attacking you. Do you know who else they're attacking? God! Because they hate God as much as they hate America. They hate our flag, they hate our freedom, and they will stop at nothing to hurt me. Tonight, for you, for our people, I'm declaring a state of emergency until we can figure out what the hell is going on." The President sat up and sniffed while he attempted to focus his dilated pupils. The President belted out one more line before his gaunt son-in-law signaled to the crew to get him off camera. "One day you will wake up and this will all have gone away. I alone can fix this and save our great nation."

The televisions zoomed in on the President's well-coiffed daughter and her husband standing behind her. He offered a smirk, and she offered shallow condolences to the broken country: "You and your family are in our thoughts and prayers as we go through this difficult time together."

The cameras panned out to the rest of the family who were still in the President's power circle and good graces. In unison they flashed plastic smiles and put their thumbs up: "The country is safe in our hands. God bless America and God Bless our great President."

The TVs went blank.

In Our Bones

Bubble of Concern

"Please, anyone! Any other human being, please, please enter!" Lauren called out into the echoing warehouse.

Nary a customer had set foot all inside the pet store all day; it was vastly different from her previous job at the Silver Lake Bar. Her co-worker, Craig, was in the back keeping to himself as usual. A few thousand nondescript feeder fish, an oversized cage of dozens of guinea pigs, a snuggling pile of bunnies, and a mama cat with kittens also occupied the building. Lauren was thinking of taking the mama cat home if the owners turned her back out on the street after the kittens were gone. Adult cats still sold occasionally to people dealing with infestations of one sort or another, so there was hope for her. Populations of feral cats and dogs had surged, and packs of street dogs were a growing menace. Wild cat colonies had further decimated already declining populations of songbirds and any other small creatures they could sink their teeth into. Animal welfare organizations were overwhelmed and barely functioning. The store's corporate parent company had long since reversed course on only selling rescue dogs and cats. It had only been a PR move anyway when times were better and bleeding hearts had enough collective power to make the world a bit less cruel.

Life in the decade since the President consolidated power had not been easy. Lauren responded by crawling so far into her shell that a tinge of misanthropy had snuck in, too. She preferred working with animals than humans. The owners treated them like chattel, but she did her best to care for them when she was working. Her hours were continually shrinking, though, and they posted their number on the door for shoppers to call if they needed anything. This practice had become common in all but the busiest stores, as everyday conveniences for ordinary people gradually eroded. The seemingly natural flow of wants and needs from point to point had broken down. All but the youngest remembered the days before the pandemic with bittersweet nostalgia when merely existing wasn't a hustle. The bedraggled middle class had shrunk down to a sliver and missed the days when the highways were good, and garbage was collected reliably. For many Americans, the decline felt sudden and unexpected. They found it virtually incomprehensible how their lives had slid so far, so fast. Those grappling with poverty, disabilities, and discrimination before the collapse suffered even more because of it. The American Dream never lived up to its ideals for everyone, and they were much less taken by surprise, perceiving the decline as yet another floorboard breaking in an house with a caved-in roof.

Lauren's work hours were so few on some days that by the time she paid for the gas to get to and from it was almost a losing proposition. Living in town would make getting to work cheaper, but Lauren preferred the relative safety of her country home. At that moment, though, Lauren's biggest worry was this store would join the rest of the strip in collecting graffiti and the ever-burgeoning population of homeless people.

Elbows bent on the store's counter, she called out with a forlorn voice, "Just come and buy some dog food, people!"

It was crazy windy outside, and she didn't expect anyone to venture out anyway. She became lost in thoughts of her latest boyfriend when the door chimed. Lauren looked up to see two men, younger and older mirror images of one another. They both wore jeans, button down shirts and rumpled ball caps. Lauren straightened herself up and smiled. She welcomed them with a lilt in her voice, imaging she'd summoned them with her entreaties.

"Hi, what can I help you with today?" In those days, store cultures mostly went one of two ways – completely ignoring potential shoppers until their wallets came out or over-serving them out of desperation. Lauren tended toward the latter.

The older man caught her off guard when he gazed knowingly at her. "Aren't you Dale Hansberry's daughter?"

At the sound of her father's name, she stifled a small smile. But having this stranger know who she was unnerved her. "Yep, that's right."

"I was so sorry when he went. Your dad was one of the finest men I ever knew," the older man lamented.

After her father's death, another part of Lauren had disintegrated. She hadn't really appreciated him until he was gone. Lauren fought off the urge to shed a few grief-tinged tears of pride and swallowed hard at the lump in her throat.

"Thank you, sir. That's kind of you to say. I don't think we've met, though. How do you know me?"

"No, no. We haven't met. My name is Jack Fitzpatrick." He reached out to shake her hand and pulled it back, embarrassed. Without a functional health infrastructure in the country, illness continued to run unchecked. Handshaking had gone by the wayside, but many still found the instinct hard to break. "This is my boy, Sam." He nodded to the boyish man standing next to him. "Your dad would sometimes share pictures of you on Facebook back in the day." His expression fell into a more serious pose. "Dale was so honored to be your father."

A strand of emotional intimacy drifted into the moment that took Lauren aback. This stranger had just answered the question she'd so often pondered: was her father proud of her? She blushed and dropped her head.

"Your dad and I had coffee just about every morning with the guys at the restaurant way back. When he was gone, the light of reason went out of it all. I had to quit going. I sure do miss him." His expression became grave as he stated quietly, "All those guys carrying on about stuff... it was just so... you know..." he trailed off. "They just shouldn't have been talking that way."

Lauren sucked in her breath as she braced for more and released it in relief as she realized that Jack was not going to get into it. She understood perfectly what Jack had meant, but she did not at all want to talk about any of it. Lauren was still trying to stay neutral in a world where doing so meant complicity. She was working to construct a response when Jack's somber tone vanished, and he put his mask of congeniality back on. "Anyway, enough about that," his voice had an upward cadence as if he had a direction he was aiming for. "I need to get a few of those guinea pigs over there."

"Yes. Of course." She replied as she ushered them over to the enclosure and shook her head as she was taking all of this in after so many years of not thinking of her father's words.

"I'll take five. Just pick out whichever ones you can grab," Jack chuckled. "But I'll be back if I don't get a few boys and girls. I'm planning to breed them."

Sam had been such a wallflower he had been only marginally present, until he wasn't. His clear blue eyes connected with Lauren's and he blurted out unexpectedly, "You know we're going to eat them, don't you? Well, maybe not those ones. But we're adding guinea pigs to the farm. It's a good source of protein."

Prior to this interaction, Lauren had somehow not connected the dots with why everyone was suddenly buying all the guinea pigs. She felt the earth shift beneath her as she took in what he was saying. He also annoyed her, since talking about the things done for survival was not considered polite conversation.

His dad looked hard at him. "Is that really necessary? Let her do her job."

The silence was broken, though both Jack and Lauren pretended that he hadn't said it. Sam charitably let it drop. Back at the register the lot of guineas rang up to more than Jack had. His face colored, and he turned to Sam. "Son, do you have some cash? Looks like I'm a little short. I thought they were selling for less?" Jack mumbled into the ether.

"I'm sorry, Mr. Fitzpatrick, but the price is always changing. That's why we don't put signs on the cages anymore. We just never know."

Sam reached into his pocket and pulled out a threadbare twenty. As functional government had been hollowed out and replaced with political appointees, all administrative functions were failing. For the Treasury Department it had begun over a decade before when the nationwide coin shortage hit during the pandemic. By this point they weren't replacing worn money and frazzled bills remained in circulation. There was no consensus on when a bill was too worn to be money anymore, so Lauren had to use her best judgment as a cashier. She usually accepted whatever was given, even though the owners were sometimes angry. Lauren didn't want to embarrass anyone or make their lives harder than they already were. It was one little thing she could do for the world, she reasoned.

Sam told Jack without condescension, "Keep it."

Lauren found herself drawn to these men and grinning at the ease between them. Before they left, Jack turned to Lauren. "Ya know, if there's ever anything you need, look me up." He scribbled his contact info on a scrap of paper from his pocket. "My wife Rosa would just love you. She remembers Dale. We're into plants like he was. He said you were, too. And, how's your sister? Rachel?"

Lauren examined the address he'd given her and sidestepped the question about Rachel. They barely spoke. "Yeah, I like to fiddle around outside. It looks like we live really close to each other. I think I've driven by there. You've got that huge maple in the front, right?"

"That's the place. Well, I'll leave you to it. But you've got my number and remember that my door is always open."

Lauren watched as they bent against the wind. Lauren braced against a rush of emotion. Jack had inadvertently brought to the surface a multitude of sore points, and Lauren could not handle processing it. She shoved the thoughts away into their little drawers in her mind and turned her attention to the creepiness of the guinea pig conversation. She was horrified thinking about their teensy carcasses roasting in a hot dish pan, but she also realized that it wasn't much different than rabbits, or chicken, or any other farm animal for that matter. Meat is meat. Still, the topic would be something Craig would find amusing. He'd been friendlier with her lately, and she'd gotten a glimpse of a wry humor that matched her own. She locked the front doors and posted her cell number in the window in case anyone else came.

Lauren found Craig on the concrete floor with a clipboard in his hand, sorting through a ragged collection of miscellanies. Lauren walked with a little swagger to her step as she savored the thought of his reaction.

Craig saw her as she came in and smiled politely.

Lauren turned on her charm and bubbled out, "Hey, Craig. You'll never guess what just happened."

He raised his eyebrow and said with deadpan sarcasm. "What? Tell me."

Lauren felt glee that she had indeed broken through. "It's so freaky. These guys I know, or kinda know... I guess they knew my dad, or the dad knew my dad..."

Craig put up his hand in exasperation. "Lauren. Girl. You're killing me. What happened?"

"These guys just bought guinea pigs to eat. They're starting a guinea pig farm, I guess. Did you realize that's what we're doing now? Selling mini fucking livestock!"

Craig guffawed, "Oh my word, that's disgusting. Seriously? I mean, for real, they said that? I can't even..." He whispered inaudibly, "America's certainly great now."

"Let's see if we can search it. We'll be better informed for the customers, right?" Lauren squeaked, hoping the on-again-off-again internet would be functioning.

Craig picked up his phone. "Alright. Here we go." His large brown eyes danced while he scrolled. "You cannot be serious! There is so much crap on here about eating guinea pigs! That's just freaking crazy. Have we really come to this?" His question was serious, but his tone was bouncy. Still, Lauren detected the tiniest bit of sadness under his laughter.

He patted the floor and said, "Want to watch a video?"

Lauren joined him as they watched a video after video on husbandry of the small rodent. Craig's giggles were infectious, and Lauren was clinging to that joy after her unsettling interaction with Jack. Humor was the last shelter when her soul was troubled, and fun was as scarce a commodity as anything else in those days. After moving on from the videos, they watched others with kitty cats playing and pigs and goats who were friends – all approved for release as non-threatening to State power and authority. They laughed until they exhausted themselves, as they rolled back to cradle their heads on a stack of empty boxes and fell silent. Lauren's thoughts turned to her boyfriend at home and her hopes that love would last this time.

She heard a whimper that brought her back to the moment and peered at Craig as grief wracked his body. He started whispering, "It's not coming back. None of it. The old world will never come back." His chest quivered with small spasms and quiet tears flowed down his face and into his curly hair.

Lauren instinctually wanted to turn away from him, to give him privacy. She scarcely knew him, and the depths of his grief sent fear rippling through her chest.

She pushed herself to remain present. She may have been cool at times, but she refused to be an ice queen like her mom. She reached out a clumsy hand and rubbed his head, trying to soothe him.

"I'm sorry. I'm so sorry." Craig began to sob profusely and turned away.

Lauren sat up and cradled herself, unsure what she should do until she spotted a roll of the store's rough toilet paper. She brought it back to him and stayed quiet, since no words could come to her lips no matter how she tried.

After a long while, Craig rolled over and Lauren handed him the tissue. His voice was barely audible. "Thanks." He regrouped slowly, and Lauren laid back down next to him.

"Is there anything I can do? Do you want to talk about it?"

"I do want to talk, but I'm scared. I don't know if I can trust you."

Lauren panicked, what if he was going to tell her something horrible, like if he'd murdered someone or stole money from the store. She hid her grimace and assured, "You can trust me."

"Are you sure you're safe?"

Now Lauren was really starting to worry, but the fear in Craig's eyes had pulled her into his pain. She had to bear witness to whatever he had to say. "Of course," she murmured in her most soothing voice.

"I want to talk to you, but I need to know that you won't tell anyone. And I mean no one." Lauren nodded in agreement. His voice was gravelly as he spoke. "I'm not really Craig. I mean, I was born Craig. But my name is *really* Sophie. I was living as her for four years, through most of high school, even. I was so worried that my parents would disown me. Especially my dad. He wasn't thrilled, but he was fine. His biggest thing was all the Black trans girls getting killed. We seemed to have it the worst. But I told him that I was dying inside, living a lie..."

Lauren had no idea. She was shocked since she'd never known any trans people before. She did understand the danger that Sophie was describing, though. Dale had ranted about the queer purges before he died. She didn't know the details but had been horrified when she heard. She shuddered and realized she'd forgotten all about her own problems. Sophie broke down again, and Lauren handed her more tissue.

After a time, a wistful expression fell over Sophie's face.

"My mom had only sons, so she was thrilled. My friends were a little weirded out, but cool. My mom took me shopping, and we got my hair done in a gorgeous weave. The stylist said I looked like Beyoncé. I even got my nails done long with sparkles. I was beautiful. Every day I woke up and was finally happy to see myself in the mirror, even if some people were assholes. The people who mattered were supporting me…"

When Sophie cried again, her tears were raw. Scalding. Lauren found the strength to move in closer and rub her back when Sophie rolled into a ball. Lauren checked her phone and it was well past closing time. It didn't really matter as her man of the moment would be out with his friends. She propped herself up on her elbow as Sophie began again after another half hour or more. Lauren resisted the urge to play on her phone.

"I lived out and proud until it got so scary. I was still living at home because it was really hard to get a job. All those kids who harassed me in school knew where I was. They started driving past the house, throwing shit in the yard. I thought my dad was going to have a heart attack. He'd marched for civil rights back in his day, and he came so far that he joined PFlag and marched in the last Pride we got to hold. I think it broke his heart more than Mom's when I went back to him. Back to… Craig!" She spat the name with contempt and rolled her mouth around as if she were tasting bile. Sophie looked Lauren straight in the eye. "I had to send Sophie away to stay alive, Lauren. That's my deadly secret. I had to send her away." Sophie's entire body trembled, and she cried longer than anyone Lauren had ever sat with.

Lauren bristled at her own discomfort. *Rachel would know what to do*, she thought. She'd only ever known a few gay guys from work at the restaurant. It seemed like all her girlfriends in high school were pansexual or bi or some other thing that Lauren didn't entirely understand, either. She wondered what had happened to all of them and stifled it quickly. She couldn't save them. She couldn't save Sophie. She was barely saving herself. She took comfort knowing she could keep Sophie's story safe. Lauren tried to calm her. "I'm so sorry, Sophie. I'm so very sorry for what you've been through."

Sophie snapped, "Don't call me that ever again. I thought I could trust you."

Lauren was confused. "You can. But isn't that who you said you were? I was trying to be supportive."

"I know you were, but it shows that you don't get it. It's not safe, Lauren. You can never use that name again. Do you hear me? Then maybe I can live long enough to one day be her again. Maybe this could still all blow over somehow, and we can all try to be happy again."

Lauren reeled and wiped at her eyes. "I know. I didn't mean to upset you. I won't ever call you that again. I'll never say anything. Please trust me."

"I'm not sure that I can. But I want to. I'm an empath, or at least that's what my aunt says. She told me I'm like her; we can sense what people are feeling. Sense what's in their heart. I think you're that way, too. I felt it right away when we met. That's why I told you, I guess. I haven't said anything to anyone since I went back in the closet. Damnit, girl. I better be able to trust you." She laughed a weak and small puff of air.

Lauren considered what she'd said about her, and she didn't agree. Lauren spent most of her time trying to keep everyone else's feelings at bay, but she was glad that Sophie had confidence in her. Lauren said, "I won't tell a soul. I'm glad you told me; I was so worried about you." Sophie was more relaxed, at an existential level, than Lauren had ever seen her. Lauren realized that she'd never actually seen *her* until now, though.

Sophie's face lit up. "It felt good to tell someone. Maybe one day you'll meet her. Meet Sophie, I mean. She was one hell of a lady! Until then, I never want to hear that name come outta your mouth. Okay?"

"Okay, I promise." Lauren grinned.

"How about we put those animals to bed and get out of here?" Sophie smiled and got up from the floor.

Lauren was surprised when Sophie embraced her. Lauren was unaccustomed to hugs, and most felt as stiff and cold as her father's corpse at his funeral. On the rare occasions when she saw Rachel, her nephew gave sweet squeezes with his little arms. Sophie's hug was expansive and reminded her of hugs from when she was a child, from when she didn't hold back her heart. Lauren melted into her.

Lauren only worked with Sophie a few more shifts. She never knew what happened after that and was too terrified to find out.

Party Related Hoopla

A glossy anachronistic party invitation was thrust into Lauren's face along with the words, "I hope you can come."

Claudia beamed as bright as the sunlight pouring through the large windows of the pet store. The card was adorned with the image of a graduate wearing a gown and tossing his cap into the air. Claudia was now the only other employee besides Lauren left at the Pet Depot. She had an effervescent nature and frequently brought in little treats for Lauren.

"Where on earth did you get these things?" Lauren teased while looking at the invite. Her eyes twinkled at fond memories of childhood parties with colorful balloons and sticky frosting.

"I cleaned out the Dollar Store years ago before they shut down. Most parents dream of their kids' wedding. I suppose I always pinned my hopes on his graduation party, since who knows if he'll ever get married. He's so serious and keeps to himself so much I worry about him. But anyway, these cards were on clearance along with a bunch of other stuff. They've been living in my basement since then. You know I only took this job so I could get my kids through private school. The school they'd been going to was such a mess, we didn't have a choice if we wanted them to actually get an education…"

Claudia trailed off, her eyes searching for a future she could no longer imagine. Lauren knew that Claudia always thought her son would go to the Ivy League. No one talked about that anymore, things being what they were.

Sensing sorrowing gathering in Claudia, Lauren swatted her with a towel and laughed, "It's going to be the best party in town, so you'd better quit handing out the invitations. You'll be overrun."

Claudia giggled and grabbed the towel away from Lauren and clipped her with it. Lauren loved that Claudia could joke around and was tired of dealing with people who took themselves too seriously. Lauren watched as she went off to tidy the store. Claudia was a resourceful woman, seemingly able to will her way toward order and success. She could make the crumpled brown food bags and scattered odds and ends look almost like a real store again.

Lauren worried about Claudia and decided that she should offer her assistance. Claudia seemed like the kind of person who was there for everyone else, but there weren't many there for her. Lauren had no doubt

Claudia would pull off an amazing party, even if graduation parties were sparser than ever, but she would still need help. As society fractured, families worked together more to make sure important things got done. Graduation parties were still on the list of important things.

Still, many kids were dropping out of school to find work in the glutted labor pool. Some universities still functioned and good jobs existed for a lucky few. But college was no longer the goal for most families as their kids accepted whatever work they could find, took up trades or gave up, retreating into their parent's basements. Lauren's own transition to adulthood had been rocky enough; she grieved for the life these kids would never have. Suicides among all ages had skyrocketed, but especially among the young who often saw few prospects. Lauren felt an odd sense of guilt when she'd hear of a death, as if she herself had failed them. Rachel would say that suicide was a symptom of our collective failure to care for our own, not the blame of individual around the person who died. Lauren wasn't sure about all that, but she was sure that with each suicide she'd hear about, some little piece of her died too; all the while she struggled to keep herself from succumbing.

The day of the party, Lauren resolved to not be late as usual. She headed out to the Jeep she'd been piecing together, rusted and loud. She was proud to be making it out the door on time when she caught a car pulling into her driveway. She could already guess who it was and prepared herself for the onslaught of proselytism. Lauren believed in Jesus, just not the version that so many seemed to be peddling. Even her family's church had become too much, if she were being honest with herself. Lauren's God was one of love and light.

A middle-aged man and twenty-something woman pulled up in a battered sedan. Lauren spied his shiny red tie and her button-up blouse as they got out. They were all delighted smiles for having caught a prospect out and about. The man started first, coughing to clear his throat - the seemingly omnipresent smoke from forest fires in the north being particularly thick that day.

"Excuse me, ma'am, but we're here to spread the word that the end of times are upon us," he proclaimed in a long drawled accent. He swayed his arms towards the ground as if he was summoning the Apocalypse. "You must take Jesus into your heart as your personal Lord and Savior with me now or suffer the wrath of the Lord." Anger and desperation mingled together in his voice.

Missionaries no longer trifled with niceties and benign preambles. The competition for converts and their money was fierce. They spewed their blather at anyone they could get to stand still long enough to listen.

Some newly sprouted churches strictly adhered to one faith tradition or another. But so often, they mixed and matched whatever religion, spiritual idea, or new age fantasy they could to help them stand out from the pack and catch the right person on the right day to bring them into the fold. Difficult times had everyone grasping for answers, including Lauren. Although she was searching more in matters of the heart than the soul.

Lauren tapped her foot in impatience and crossed her arms over her chest. She tried to be kind, but firm. "I already have a church. But thank you." She didn't want to leave until they'd driven off, having heard rumors of ransacked homes.

The man pushed on, "The Four Horsemen are coming, little missy. And you'd better ask yourself if you're ready!" He wagged his plump finger at her as his moon-shaped face reddened.

The woman howled, "It's in the scripture! It's in the scripture!" She held her palms open with her arms raised and shaking.

She seemed possessed for a moment, and Lauren hoped she wouldn't start speaking in tongues like the last one had. As suddenly as she began, the shouting stopped, and the woman produced pamphlets from her bag. She handed them to Lauren, who reached out to grab them, instantly annoyed with herself for having done so. The woman had a frailty to her that invoked

Lauren's pity. Knowing better, yet acting anyway, Lauren reached into her purse and pulled out a handful of bills, almost without value due to inflation. She hoped a donation would assuage them. Lauren hadn't meant to toss the money, but neither reached out fast enough, and she couldn't stop her fingers from flicking it away. Lauren was quite done with the entire situation. The heat roiling off the driveway was making her even more irritable than she'd have been otherwise. "Please. I need you to leave now," she stated flatly.

As the man squatted down to pick up the bills, and the woman gently plucked back her pamphlets, accurately sensing that she was not to gain a convert any time soon. Most missionaries had quotas to meet and had to supply their own materials for the job.

"Thank you, ma'am. We'll be back around to check on you," the man said with an ominous grin as they headed for the car.

"May you find the light, miss," the woman said sincerely before she climbed into the passenger seat. May you find the light, too, Lauren thought as their car sped away.

Claudia lived on the edge of town in a valley occupied by both newer construction and magnificent old farms. The new houses hadn't fared weather extremes well and many were in various states of significant disrepair. Lauren turned down the narrow winding road to

Claudia's house when she spotted the broken bridge ahead. It had been replaced no more than a decade before, and Lauren hadn't realized it was out again. It laid in a gash of earth like a skewed teeter totter. Lauren could see where animals and people on foot had been jumping over the crevice to the other side. But she'd have to drive back and around. Sonofabitch. So much for being on time! Working in Lauren's favor, expectations of her punctuality were crumbling along with the roadways.

As Lauren pulled in, she observed the sprawling crowd scattered across the lawn, and the fresh party decor. Unlike all the spartan, potluck celebrations around town that year, Claudia was serving real food. Lauren didn't see Claudia at first but could see much to be done. She started bagging trash and refilling snack bowls. When Claudia emerged from the kitchen looking flushed, she flashed Lauren a taut smile.

"Did you invite all these people?" Lauren asked.

Claudia replied breathlessly, "No. You were right about being overrun! I've gone into a code red to make the food stretch. I can't imagine turning anyone away, but I certainly hope no one else comes." She slipped back into the steamy kitchen as Lauren followed behind.

Claudia's air conditioning unit was on the fritz and they couldn't find the parts to fix it. A young girl with a wee head sat on a stool at the sink scrubbing potatoes.

The girl grinned at Lauren. Claudia whispered, "Her mom got Zika while she was pregnant when they were living down in Arkansas. Poor baby." Mounds of shrunken potatoes and carrots from last year's harvest piled on the counter. "Can you help Sarah wash these? I'm going to sauté them and add it to the meat. Make sure you get off all the sand, alright?"

Lauren said, "You're lucky to have all this extra food on hand."

"I know. I hadn't thought much about it before. Obviously, people are hungry, otherwise why would they be here?" Lauren took stock of how blessed she was and said a prayer for the party guests.

Lauren, Sarah, and Claudia threw together a massive plate of burgers for the grill while Claudia's husband lollygagged with his buddies. As Claudia handed him the tray, all he said was, "Thanks, sweetie." Lauren sneered; he clearly had no idea what they'd just pulled off.

The women scrambled to bring out plates and bowls brimming with delectable items as the partygoers swarmed. No one was waiting for the burgers to be cooked or for the congratulatory speeches. The party was beginning to feel more like a soup kitchen. Groceries still lined store shelves, but money to purchase them was scarce. The mix of available items was erratic and unstable, regardless. So many cogs in the wheels of the global agricultural system had come off around the same time. America had been spared the worst of the famines, but emptiness gnawed in their bellies all the same. Many farmers turned toward feeding their neighbors, rather than growing for large agribusinesses, and nearly everyone kept a garden like in the days of Victory Gardens in days of old. This time no one was so foolhardy as to believe triumph lay ahead, though, and Endurance Gardens didn't have quite the same sweet ring to it.

Lauren continued working hard throughout the party, though she'd wanted to stop. She hadn't expected the day to be so long and hard. The one saving grace was the cute guy who kept hitting on her throughout the day. Bryan was part of a group of rowdy stragglers who'd lingered on the far end of the patio near a dying corpse of river birch trees. He charmed her each time she came near, even helping fold up tables and chairs with her. She'd recently broken it off with another and was excited by the attention. Though she hadn't given him her number and to her disappointment he didn't ask.

When the clean-up was mercifully complete, Lauren shouted out a final "Congratulations" to Claudia's mostly distracted son. She was thinking of the sweet relief of sitting down in her Jeep when Bryan walked up stealth behind her.

"You done workin' already?" he said loudly, intentionally to startle.

Lauren whipped around, but when she recognized him, she relaxed. "Yeah, whatever. I didn't see you doing much."

"I was just enjoying the party, is all," he retorted, moving in a little closer than it seemed like he should, but not so close as to cause alarm. Or at least, for her to feel like she had the right to be alarmed. "I think we could enjoy some time together, too. You want to head on down to the river tomorrow? They've got some good skipping stones down there."

More than anything, Lauren wanted a man who was authentic. A man who was attentive and didn't play games. Modern dating had worn her out, with all the pretext and demands to act as disinterested as possible. No one wanted to be vulnerable. She could see that Bryan wanted her and something about his desire to skip stones together seemed like the most romantic and genuine date Lauren could imagine.

Mocking

Lauren and Bryan hiked across the field toward the lush banks of Bear Creek. That innocent trickle of water turned into a rampage that would level everything in its path on a regular basis. It hadn't flooded yet that year and was pretty, except for the rotting trailer park a few hundred yards off. Lauren knew a few people who used to live there. Aside from the carcasses of mobile homes, a handful of pull-behind campers occupied any open spot. They'd drive away when the floods came and come back to the soupy mosquito-infested mess when they returned. Revulsion nestled into her as she thought of living that way. She didn't dwell on the thought, as her attention was caught by a mama and papa mallard duck pair with babies. Their slight bodies bobbled in the gently flowing current.

Bryan climbed down a steep bank and helped Lauren down. She was impressed at his chivalry. Along the eroded walls of the creek small colorful stones tumbled along by the water's edge. Bryan picked around the bits of plastic chip bags, aluminum beer cans and other detritus to select four flat smooth rocks. He cradled them in his hands and cocked his head.

"You ready for this? You'll be impressed," he chortled.

Lauren snickered, "We'll see. Are you gonna hold those or show me something?" She ran her fingers through her hair and batted her eyes.

"I can show you something, if you want," he smirked.

Lauren bit her lip. "Get on with it, then."

Bryan put the others in his pocket and held onto a muted red stone as he instructed, "Hold it flat like this, you see? Then flick your wrist." Bryan let the rock fly and it jumped one, two, three times.

Lauren clapped. "I want to try. I never have."

"What? Well, let me help you with that. I'm a patient teacher."

Bryan touched Lauren's hip and looked into her eyes. She was mesmerized as he placed the stone in her palm and guided her hand. She tossed it out and it splashed in with no bounce. "Aww, that was no good."

"That's fine. I'm sure you're good at many other things."

Lauren blushed. "Okay, mister. Let's focus. I'm going to get this." Within a short while she got her first skip. She felt like a magician as she watched the circles ripple out into the water.

Bryan threw his arms around her and kissed the side of her head. Lauren was disarmed at how genial and tender he was with her.

"That's beautiful. You've got this," he said. She swooned.

They stayed another hour or more. Bryan skipped multiples every time. Lauren was consistently getting one skip out, but never did get to two. They giggled and wooed the whole time. Lauren was falling in love, which tended to happen quickly for her. Though not like this. Lauren sensed something different about Bryan; he was unlike anyone else she'd been with. He so unambiguously wanted her, and his heavy innuendo wasn't said with vulgarity. He was a fine enough looking man, but it was his energy that was striking. She felt as if she'd known him her entire life in just a few short hours. Lauren could feel his edge; she just didn't think it would cut.

They decided to head to town and pick up a snack from one of the stalls along the main strip. The town was dominated by the towering architectural beauty of the Clinic. The mostly empty well-guarded buildings stood mocking those below, reminding everyone of what had been lost. The Clinic had been a flagship medical organization for generations, but when one pay structure after another folded in quick succession – Medicare, Medicaid, private insurance companies – they couldn't sustain the weight of the apparatus they had built, let alone find enough doctors and nurses, since many had been immigrants who could no longer get visas. China became the global leader of innovation with Russian backing. Since China believed that their star could only rise if America's burned out, they were largely behind the international conspiracy to elect the American President. The Russian dictator and the Chinese dictator were both keen to destabilize the country and sabotaging democracy was an easy way to accomplish that task. Russia became a happy lapdog to China's egregious juggernaut so long as their dictator could keep raking in mob cash, while letting his own people starve. Everywhere the Chinese dictator's influence rose, oppression and imprisonments followed, including in the United States.

Bryan and Lauren drove into the center of town past a menagerie of vehicles, motorcycles, and bicycles. As they got closer, tents and shanties lined the streets. The evening weather was pleasant as they parked and walked the rest of the way. They stopped and gazed at this and that as they strolled along. Bryan put out his arm, and Lauren took it, feeling safe. Despite the poverty, there was a certain vibrancy to the scene that hadn't existed before when everyone was ensconced within their own comfortable existences. The market seemed to stretch forever, with vendors hocking bright baskets, clothing and trinkets. Others were selling stacks of fresh tomatoes or cucumbers, and still more were offering prepared foods. Even with what little money people had, they still didn't like to cook or even know how. Bryan seemed interested in the same things that she was, which struck her as oddly coincidental. She brushed the worry aside, choosing to look at it as kismet.

"Can we get one of those?" Lauren spied a shrunken man selling small cakes.

"Whatever you want." Bryan pulled out his wallet, sparing them the awkwardness about who would pay. Another point in his favor.

The man handed them each a dense white cake drizzled with pink frosting. Bryan told him to keep the change. As they walked away, Lauren swore that the cake seller had been her history teacher. Her eyes met his and a fierce shiver went down her spine as it seemed like everything he was feeling was transferred into her. He jerked his gaze away. As they walked away Lauren couldn't block the image of his eyes and the feeling of connection she'd had. His embarrassment was her own, and she was unsettled by the interaction. She wanted to say to him, Hey, none of our lives have turned out the way we wanted. Instead she put her arm back through Bryan's as they roamed to find a place to sit.

Bryan directed them to a low wall across from a teenage boy and delicate small girl. The children sat amidst what Lauren presumed were the last of their possessions. The boy's eyes pleaded with passers-by, hoping to make a sale. The girl smiled at Lauren, who hadn't yet gotten over the jolt from earlier when a great sadness took hold. Lauren grasped the wall and a tear leaked from the corner of her eye. She wiped it discretely and was grateful for the distraction when Bryan started talking.

"What do you think of this cake, huh?" He hadn't noticed that she'd not yet taken a bite.

Lauren wanted to get back before sundown, not feeling safe in town after dark. Bryan tried to convince her that it wasn't as bad as she thought, but she wasn't interested in finding out. As they drove back to Lauren's house, she glowed. She couldn't remember having a more perfect first date. The attraction that had been building all day burst open as they pulled into her driveway. Bryan's hands moved up and down her legs as he kissed her.

"Let's take this inside," Lauren beckoned.

Bryan followed her into the house. In her bedroom, Lauren began mechanically removing her clothing as she habitually did. She was no stranger to sex, but she'd never learned how to tap into her heart whenever she was with someone. As she kissed him, her raw feelings from the marketplace mingled with an intensity for Bryan. She found herself quietly weeping.

Bryan looked at her, evidently puzzled. "What's going on?"

Lauren was self-conscious and felt intolerably vulnerable. "It's nothing, really." She hid her face.

"It doesn't look like nothing. Tell me."

Lauren's mind raced. She wasn't sure what exactly was wrong. Nothing had happened, it was just feelings for people she even didn't know and hopes of feelings for another who she didn't know either. Lauren was confused and sat down on the bed. "I'm so embarrassed. I can't believe I'm crying. I really like you, is all. Come over here."

Bryan sat down, and she started kissing him. Lauren channeled her feelings into making love to Bryan as she'd never made love to anyone before. She let herself trust him and soaked into his warmth. After that night, things progressed quickly between them. He wasn't the first man to live with Lauren; she'd had several others. No one had brought every worldly possession inside with as much speed as Bryan, however. He was running on full octane.

Lauren was head over heels and didn't try to put on the brakes. She believed that she'd found her one true love at long last, a knight in his decrepit Chevy. When Lauren texted Rachel about him, her sister had been concerned. It pissed Lauren off. For once, she was happy and felt that her life was going the direction it was supposed to. Lauren was certain Rachel would like him if she met him. But after that text, she shut out her sister completely. She couldn't deal with the judgment anymore. Lauren loved Rachel's boy, Ben, but she hardly saw him anyway. It pulled at her each time she saw him regardless, knowing it would be a long while until she saw him again. It reminded her of Rachel leaving her when she was young, and that brought more bad memories. It was easier to take a break.

The first months together were amazing. They'd gone back to the creek, and Lauren got a few double skips. They drank and sat outside together; he helped with chores and did kind things for her. Lauren felt that she was his one and only. She was so sure this time. When Bryan's cruelty began to reveal itself, she hardly noticed at first as he would pass it off as a joke. If Lauren reacted, she was just being too sensitive, he'd say. His critiques of her housekeeping and the way she dressed followed. When they argued, he'd insist that he hadn't said horrible things Lauren had heard him say. Lauren could not reconcile the person Bryan became with who he had been, since the change had been so gradual. He insisted that the problems lay with her. He'd be warm one second then shift to an emotional assault that he'd deny later. Other times he'd push Lauren's buttons until she'd explode then say that she was unstable. She was a mess. The same energy Bryan used to reel her in was now being used to manipulate her. Lauren was left feeling drained and confused, wishing things could magically return to the way they'd been in the beginning.

Disagreeing with Bryan became untenable as his version of reality was the only valid one. By the time he began accusing her of sleeping around and searching her phone, she was in so deep that she didn't know which way was up. He'd lost his job and began hanging out with the group of guys he'd known since he was a kid. Lauren noticed that Bryan began sprinkling in racist and anti-female rants about the same time. Before long, he was with his old buddies three or four nights a week. Lauren didn't ask questions about what they were doing. Bryan didn't offer. When Bryan would go off, Lauren would think of her family. Her father and sister would have been appalled.

Lauren's nephew was bi-racial, and when Rachel found out Lauren voted for the President, she was incensed. "How could you?" she asked. Lauren finally connected the President's words to the country he'd created.

Lauren felt as if she was a passenger in her own life as Bryan's fury grew. He'd begun punching the wall next to her or raising his fist. Lauren was certain he would strike her soon and felt powerless. The President ruled by executive order and overturned laws recognizing domestic violence as a crime. Lauren believed that she had no way to make it out alive. She couldn't make him leave. She had no one to help her make him leave. At times, her despair grew so dark that she could barely imagine living another day. Suicide ran in her family, and she'd nursed thoughts of her own demise for as long as she could remember.

When she was young, she'd sneak over to the decaying turkey barns that had bankrupted the grandpa she'd never known. Her mom didn't like her to be there since that was that spot where he'd put a bullet through his heart. Lauren would lie in the grass between the tall round buildings where no one could see her. The wind would whip through the hollow buildings, and she would imagine herself being carried up in the gusts and blow away into nothing. She wanted to disappear more than die. Nowadays, death itself had a singular appeal. She sometimes went into the kitchen and opened the drawer to gaze at the thin curved blade of her tomato knife. Lauren would run her finger along the razor-sharp tip as she imagined it slipping perfectly into her jugular. She'd wince against the pain and then feel the release. She could hide the wound without Bryan suspecting. He'd found the scars on her inner thigh where, as a girl she'd slice neat rows, just to remember that she was real. Bryan had yelled at her, told her she was weak. Of the insults Bryan leveled at her, that one stung the worst. She may have been many things, but she was not weak.

Sometimes she felt the only reason she stayed alive was to deny him the satisfaction of her demise.

Lauren also wouldn't give him the satisfaction of knowing why she had ever started cutting herself. It all started from a single event. An event that she would try to tell herself was no big deal but would take her a lifetime to untangle. One of the few solid truths that Lauren could hold onto in her life was that after that night she was different, no matter how Eric explained it to the kids at school.

Just before Lauren turned sixteen, she snuck out of the house. She knew better and had never done anything like it before. She wasn't one to break the rules but couldn't resist. Eric was one of the most sought-after boys at school, and Lauren was determined that she would make him hers. She'd never had a real boyfriend before, had never been kissed, and she was tired of feeling like a child because of it. Lauren decided that this would be the night when she would grow up.

Eric pulled up in his ostentatious car at the end of her driveway and switched off the lights. Lauren's parents were fast asleep as she descended the creaking stairs and out the door. Her pulse raced as he said, "Climb in," and handed her a beer. Lauren could still remember the crack of the can and the bitter fizz against her tongue. She'd never drank before but kept that to herself. They sped into the cloying darkness of the moonless night as gravel rattled against the car.

"Where are we going?" she asked.

"Don't you worry about that bae, I've got a plan."

Eric urged her to drink up as he handed her another. Otherwise he barely acknowledged that she was there, prattling on about this grievance or that. "What a douchebag, you know what I'm saying?" and "I told her to go to hell," and on and on. His words swam together with the repetitive rural landscape as they drove. Eric produced a pack of cigarettes and handed her a lit one. Lauren sat there awkwardly as the acrid smoke filled the car. She took a long puff and didn't cough like they do in the movies, but the combination of the beer and the cigarette made the world start spinning. She clutched the door and tried to steady herself. Lauren barely noticed when the car slowed down and pulled onto a little side drive. Lauren was sick as he opened her door and put out his hand.

"Why are we here?"

"I just thought we'd dance a little," Eric purred as he pulled her in tight and put his hands low on her back.

"But there's no music."

Lauren tried to convince herself that this was the romantic night she'd wanted, but when he started sucking at her neck and groping her bottom, she knew that it wasn't. Still, she didn't want to come across as a hysterical child, so she forced herself to go along. Eric swayed clumsily and started grinding his hardness into her leg. Lauren's nausea and discomfort were growing as he reached his hand around and grabbed her crotch.

She pushed it away. "Eric, don't."

She tried to pull away from him as he tightened his grip. Without a word, he swept her legs from beneath her and laid Lauren down in the fine limestone dust. Tall stalks of dry corn were the only witness. Lauren's brain screamed many words, but her mouth was unable to form a sound. The smell of his body wash hung in the air. The road's rocks dug into her back, but she hardly felt the pain as her mind and body detached from the moorings that had held them together. Eric tore into Lauren as her flesh burned. She lay frozen, almost able to see the gossamer of her spirit float into the liminal space between life and death.

Eric grunted, "You're so hot," before he released inside of her. Lauren felt his ooze drain out. After, Eric laughed and said, "That was awesome."

Lauren dressed quickly, stuffing the torn panties into her pocket. They drove the few minutes back to her house in silence. Lauren realized that they'd never actually been going anywhere, her assault was the destination. By the time classes started on Monday, everyone thought they knew what had happened. Lauren couldn't offer a rebuttal because she couldn't understand everything herself. She'd chosen to go with him. She hadn't said no. She hadn't stopped him. Maybe she had wanted it, like Eric said? The incident turned to such confusion that it was pulling Lauren apart. That's when she started cutting herself, and that's when she erected the well-arranged partitions within her mind. They were walls of protection, but they also shut her away.

Lauren quietly resented her entire family for somehow not knowing what was wrong. She needed them more than anything, needed them to see her pain. She used cruel words and outbursts to shake them from their malaise, but her family only retreated behind their own walls. Feeling like an outcast, Lauren mutilated herself to mirror her interior transformation. She dyed her hair black and put on clothes that matched. Her only makeup was green lipstick that brought out the color of her eyes. To everyone else, Lauren's new look was horrifying. To her, it was a giant fuck you that signaled her disdain for everyone and everything. She maintained the look into her twenties, before she tired of the otherness of it all. She let her hair grow out over time, the dark dye contrasting sharply with the blonde.

Lauren had never told anyone what happened, and still couldn't bring herself to use the "R word" to describe it. She'd wanted to tell Bryan when they first got together, since he had made her believe that he could hold her and the weight of her suffering. But the divisions within her psyche were too high and too thick, and she didn't have the courage. Over time, anything she had disclosed was used to hurt her, and she held onto her secret more tightly than ever.

Once she'd heard Bryan and his macabre friend, Steven, talking about women and assault. Bryan opined, "It's all bullshit. They start it and then blame us. How's a man supposed to even know how to act around them anymore?"

Steven's rat-like eyes narrowed when he said, "Beware the Jezebels, Bryan. The Good Book warned us about them. Females are treacherous." Steven's girlfriend stared intently at her drink. "They want to strip of us our masculinity and our power, and that's why we need to show them their place."

An icy flush washed over her. In her trauma-driven nightmares Eric and Bryan blended seamlessly together.

In Our Bones

Pernell Plath Meier

Innumerable Particles

Lauren watched through the window as unwieldy bolts of lightning struck across the sky. Claps of thunder shook the house and combined with Bryan's incessant angry screaming. As the storms gathered outside for a third day in a row, Lauren sensed that those brewing inside were more dangerous. She'd seen Bryan's fury building. Lauren wasn't sure precisely which bees were in his bonnet, but with Bryan there were so many bees. And it seemed the only thing he put any effort into was yelling. His preference was to sit as much as possible. He most especially preferred sitting in the green recliner in Lauren's living room – the recliner where Bryan wiped his hands when he'd eat, drool when he'd sleep, and spill his seed when he watched porn on his virtual reality headset. Now that he had claimed it, Lauren despised the chair and its associated mess. She'd sneer whenever she walked by and secretly referred to Bryan as His Royal Fucking Majesty as he sat in that goddamned throne of his. She would imagine setting it on fire with him in it.

61

Lauren felt safer when he was in the chair, though. His shouted demands and denigrations could hurt her in spirit only. He'd have to get up if he wanted to do much damage beyond that. Lauren kept clear of his grasp whenever she went near him, watching his hands so she knew where they were. Whenever he insisted that she be up close – so close as to press her skin to his – Lauren felt the scorch as if she'd already set him ablaze. Making love with Bryan as she'd done in the beginning was a distant memory. He used her openness to deride her and tell her that she was a nasty slut. He'd withhold sex haphazardly, then demand it in an instant. Lauren guessed that it was all some sick game designed to break her even more.

The last months, she'd started to feel more insignificant than ever. The only time Bryan touched her was to put his prick in her mouth so that he could moan and grind to his VR porn. Lauren felt like nothing more to him than a sex toy. That day he demanded, "Bitch, get on that." Lauren's flesh crawled, but she complied. She always complied. Even so, Bryan became angry when her technique was insufficient for his need. He took off his headset and shoved her away, "You can't do anything right! You're just not fun anymore, Lauren." Contempt dripped from his lips, "Get away from me. You disgust me."

Lauren sat on the floor with her face in her hands bawling as quietly as she could. Bryan shouted at her, "Get the hell out of here! You're so loud I can't hear." Waves of hot shame roiled inside her. Lauren forced her limbs to move, as the cold and vacant space in her chest grew. She moved like a robot to the back porch for a cigarette, where the acrid smoke could keep her crumbling interior spaces from collapsing altogether. The porch was where she'd go when death was so tangible that she could feel the weight of the tomato knife in her hand. Smoking may not have been an efficient suicide, but in the end, it was all the same. Death by a thousand drags.

After sucking down enough nicotine and nips from her bottle, Lauren was numb enough to function once more. The sun was low in the sky as she trekked across the muddy yard to the barn. Lauren groaned when she saw that the daisies by the fence line were mashed down. They'd just opened their petals a few days before. Of everything she'd lost since the change, she missed the flowers the most. Nature would tatter them as soon as she brought them into the world. This ravage or that always got them before their time. Sophie's words from the pet store floated into her mind. It's not coming back. None of it.

Lauren pushed on to the barn, needing to sit down as despair took hold. At least they got to bloom. She plopped down on a straw bale as another flood of tears came.

Lauren felt the pokey straw under her leg and heard the impatient clucks, neighs, and bleats of her livestock. She wanted them to be fed, but she did not want to be the one to feed them – not tonight. She wanted to sit. She wanted to rest for once, like His Highness sat every night. The goats knocked at the gate with their hooves and the horses pranced in their stalls. Lauren would normally call out their names as she hurried with their food, but her limbs were like lead.

A colorful rooster flew down from his perch in the rafters and made her jump. She let loose. "The fuck is wrong with you, scaring me like that? I don't care if you're hungry! I'm tired, and I'm sick of every one of you!"

Lauren's eyes grew wide as she couldn't believe the words tumbling from her lips. Through everything, she'd loved her animals. She looked down and kicked at the dirt floor, realizing that the walls cutting her off from normal feelings were near complete. She would be as cold as Ann soon. The rooster strutted about looking silly. A crooked smile fell across Lauren's face. I wonder what dad would say if I asked, "Is wanting to set fire to Bryan enough reason to not work?" Chuckling softly, she finally got up. Lauren couldn't ignore the critters.

The sky opened up and rain beat loudly against the metal roof. Lauren opened the barn door and watched the deluge. It was coming down in heavy sheets, almost like the dumping buckets from the pools she went to as a kid. Wisconsin Dells, Waterpark Capital of the World, was just a few hours away and made for a cheap vacation before they all shut down. The water would pour out so hard that it felt like it would fill up her eye sockets if she tried to keep looking. Lauren would always keep her head down and eyes shut tight, as she learned to do with most everything else. Something was shifting inside her that day, however. She was feeling things, and it was spreading. Lauren was having episodes like this all the time. They'd started on that first date with Bryan and would come up at unexpected times that she couldn't suppress. The episodes were getting worse and more intense each time. Lauren was afraid that she was going crazy.

Bryan had taken things too far that day, and Lauren could not push the feelings away. She kept picturing his pants around his ankles and his smug face. As she stared at the wall of water coming down, she couldn't hold it in any longer.

She screamed, "You don't even know what love is! You are such an asshole, Bryan. Hurting me won't fix what's broken in you."

The harder the wall of water came down, the louder were her screams. She flipped off the deluge and stomped her feet like the child he had always accused her of being. Droplets gathered on the dusty floor, soaking the fraying edge of her jeans. Lauren threw her head high and howled a vast visceral cry, as if the pain in her voice could transform him into the person she thought he was, or change her into someone he might actually love. She dropped to her knees, smashing the ground until her fists were bruised, and the rain dissipated. Exhausted, Lauren dusted herself off - finally ready to face Bryan again. As she opened the door to her house, her blood turned to ice in an instant. He was sitting at the kitchen table looking straight at her. He was not in his recliner, and Lauren didn't know what was coming. She avoided eye contact as she took off her coat and boots. She steadied herself against the wall to wait.

Bryan's sarcastic voice split the silence. "You sure took your sweet time, didn't you? What were you doing out there?"

"What do you mean? I was taking care of the animals. What do you think I was doing?" Lauren worried that he'd heard her yelling. She bit her lip.

The veins pulsed in his neck. "I don't know, Lauren. But here's what I do know. You've been a real cunt lately, thinking you can just do whatever you want. Do you realize how lucky you are to have me? No one else could ever love you. Your own family didn't even love you, did they? Where's this sister of yours, huh? She's not here, Lauren, because she doesn't care. The reality is that I'm the only one who will ever love you, and I can barely stand you. You need discipline because like all women, you're weak. You need leadership and a firm hand to show you the light. It's not your fault I've been too lax. It's mine, Lauren."

He came closer. Lauren held her breath.

He grabbed her and pushed her against the wall by her throat. Lauren froze as neither fight nor flight were viable options. Bryan pressed into the soft spot of her neck, and she was sure he would kill her. She closed her eyes as his spit spattered onto her face.

"What you need is to follow the rules of Sharia. Not the Muzzie Sharia, but our own version. White Sharia. Steven's been telling me about it, and I'm convinced it's the secret to restoring harmony between us. God never meant for women to be so free, it makes a family unstable. It's in the Bible: 'Let the woman learn in silence with all subjection. But suffer not a woman to usurp authority over the man, but to be in silence.' It's time this household starts following the laws of God."

Bryan let go of her, and Lauren coughed. Her throat burned, and she could still feel his hands on her. Bryan hadn't even been religious when they got together, now he was quoting Scripture. Lauren hoped that if she kept her mouth shut, he'd let her alone, so she tried to be as nonexistent as possible. He started ranting again, "It's all in the Bible, Lauren. It tells us everything we need to know to live a good life. We are the people of Adam, and it's our duty to defend the faith against anyone who challenges it."

Lauren saw her reflection in Bryan's dead eyes as his hand pulled back.

"You're making me do this." He struck her rocklike on the side of the head, and she put her arms up in defense. Bryan glared. "You're pathetic, you know that? I know how hard it is for you to think because you have such a very little brain. I now understand that you're incapable of providing a happy home without me showing you the way. I've got a meeting with Steven. We'll talk more about this when I get home."

Bryan pushed past her and slammed the outside door behind him. Lauren heard his engine rev and wished that he'd be absorbed by the frightful weather and never return. She groped for the chair and pulled herself over to the table. She had to think. She had to get him out. How? Maybe I can pay someone? It wasn't difficult to get dirty deeds done for the right price. After they sold Lauren's family's land to a Chinese conglomerate, she had plenty of money. Though she knew she couldn't follow through on something like that, no matter how awful Bryan was. She was getting desperate enough to call Rachel. She would know what to do. Lauren's head throbbed, and she drug herself to the bedroom. She slid out of her wet pants and put on flannel PJs and crawled into bed. Pulling the blankets up tight, she tried to force her fear and shame away.

Lauren thought of her reaction to the animals in the barn earlier and didn't recognize herself. She also thought of Bryan and everyone who'd hurt her, as she felt hot indignation rise. At once, Lauren resented everyone she'd ever known so fervently that it scared her. Then as if something broke open inside of her, images and sensations without words washed over her - Bryan's spittle, Eric's body wash, her father's frail hands, Sophie's tears, the flattened daisies. Those and more ran together as each memory became indistinguishable from another, and Lauren was unable to separate which feelings were hers and which were another's. She sat up in bed, gasping for air and gripping the sheets. This episode was unlike anything she'd had before. It felt like she was separating into innumerable particles and ascending into the universe. She was everything and nothing simultaneously. Then as suddenly as the torrent of emotion began, it stopped. Lauren flung herself back on the bed dripping with sweat and mewling.

What the fuck just happened?

She thought of what Sophie had said: *We can sense what others are feeling. We can sense what's in their heart. I think you're that way, too.*

Lauren did not want to be an empath. She wanted to keep her own heart and mind nestled away and keep theirs a safe distance from her. She cried even harder at the loss of control.

What He's Capable Of

Bryan was sitting on the bed next to Lauren as his heart pounded. He'd been out all night and just returned home. He squeezed his eyes shut and wished she'd wake up on her own.

Watching Lauren sleep, Bryan noticed how beautiful she was. Her skin was soft and rosy. He'd not really looked at her for so long, he'd forgotten. She had loved him once, he knew. He also knew deep down that he was the one who ruined everything. Steven pushed him so hard that Bryan poured the rage it created onto Lauren. Bryan hoped that at least Steven would be impressed with how broken she was, because he knew that Lauren would never forgive him.

While Lauren stayed sleeping, Bryan plodded back outside. Steven, the head of the local patriot militia group, was leaning against his matte black truck. The words Defenders of the Homeland were stenciled in white on the side. Steven was mopping at his broad forehead with his permanent look of consternation.

Bryan straightened himself, since around Steven he felt meek. He wrung his hands and fumbled over his words. "Let's just leave her for now. We've got other things to do."

Steven cocked one eyebrow. His voice was flat. "Let me get this straight. You're the man of the house, right? But you're worried about disturbing your bitch? Wow, Bryan, I never saw you as a cuck."

Bryan spluttered, "I just don't want to deal with her shit, is all."

"Bryan, Bryan, Bryan..." Steven's sweat dripped. "You see, we're not going to deal with her later. And we're not going to put up with her whining. If you're too much of a fucking pussy to control your own woman, then I guess I'll have to do that for you."

Bryan shifted uncomfortably on his feet. He couldn't defy Steven now; he'd been promised a leadership position in the newly legalized group. "Fine. I'll go get her up."

"No. Don't bother now. I don't think you understand that you've demonstrated your incapacity. I've got this." Steven strode toward the house.

Bryan sprinted ahead and got to the bedroom a moment before him. Steven's malice dominated the room. His nose was thin and sharp like the rest of his body. He knocked hard on the footboard. "Wake up!"

Bryan's anxious eyes darted from Steven to Lauren. Lauren's eyes jolted open, but she lay still.

Steven barked, "Lauren! We've got some news for you. Get your ass moving, and I'll tell you all about it in the kitchen."

Lauren sat up scared. "Bryan, what is this all about?"

"Shut up." He pulled back the covers and tossed them aside. "Get dressed."

Lauren's mind raced. She wondered if she was still asleep and having a nightmare. She tried to steady her breath to keep from hyperventilating as she pulled on her clothes.

Lauren came into the kitchen to see Bryan slumped on a stool and Steven raiding the fridge with an air of entitlement. She tried to make eye contact with Bryan, but he avoided looking at her. A few months before Bryan had been bragging about Lauren's house to the guys, as if he'd built the place himself. "I've got a generator and plenty of gas still in that old farmer's tanks. I never have to stop gaming no matter what the electricity in town is doing. I've got a cellar full of food and beer, plus as much wine and corn liquor you'd ever want. Plus, the water from that deep well is so cold and clean...."

Steven's ears had perked up. He'd been hearing rumors that militia groups like the Defenders would be legalized soon and given powers of eminent domain to establish their headquarters. Bryan's mouth ran on. Militias had been growing across the country quietly for decades. Each group was independent and had their own blend of ideology. The Defender's adopted a Christian Dominionistic perspective, as developed by local resident Francis Schaeffer many years before. Schaeffer's philosophy had anti-Semitism at its core and taught that Jews were the spawn of Satan and Eve. Their hatred extended to all non-Whites and anyone not a straight cis-gendered male. When Bryan completed his induction ceremony, Steven proudly handed him a copy of The Biblical Basis for War as a manifesto of their guiding principles. Steven explained that they were all sovereign citizens not required to follow the laws of men, but only the laws of God. The Defenders stockpiled weapons and trained multiple times per week, waiting for this day to come. Random attacks had been common for a long time, and lone wolves were an ongoing threat. Though legalizing the militias was the next step in clearing the nation of undesirables.

Bryan was drawn to Steven like a moth to a searing flame. He dominated others in a way that Bryan could only dream of doing. Steven demanded and received unquestioning loyalty. In exchange, he gave his followers validation for their blind rage. It wasn't their fault that they felt less than they should. Part of Bryan knew full well what they were doing was wrong, but he couldn't let that thought come to the surface. He needed the Defenders, because for the first time in his life he felt he belonged to something. When Steven heard Bryan talk, he realized Lauren's house was perfect for what they needed. When the Attorney General announced the re-interpretation of the Second Amendment, Steven was ecstatic to move forward with his plans.

The Second Amendment had read: "A well-regulated Militia, being necessary to the security of a free State..." All the Attorney General needed to do to unleash their rage was to metaphorically remove the comma and add a teensy tiny word. He decided the Framers of the Constitution had meant, "A well-regulated Militia is necessary to the security of a free State." Paramilitary groups were given authority above local law enforcement and would answer to the President alone and added to his existing private military force. The patriot militia movement had been originally organized under the guise that they would prevent government tyranny. Once the President came to office, the movement shifted to promoting unfettered presidential power to counter demands for racial justice. An anti-government, anti-police element lurked throughout the movement as well, and attacks on officers made the profession more dangerous than ever.

Steven counted several hundred men among his forces and was ready to bring his version of justice to bear. Daily life for Americans was so chaotic that hardly anyone noticed the change to the Second, and that's what Steven was counting on. A distracted populace was far easier to control. After Steven heard Bryan boasting about Lauren's homestead, he said, "I have to say that your place sounds absolutely perfect for our new base when the time comes. When your woman is out of the house, call me and I'll inspect it. No need for her to be upset if it doesn't work for us." Steven flashed a fake smile and clapped Bryan on the back, "I'm glad to know that we've got such resourceful and loyal people as part of our family. You're a true son of the cause."

"Well, I don't know," Bryan chuckled nervously. "It's not an office or anything. Just a regular house. I don't think..." He felt faint.

Steven kept his hand on Bryan's back as he spoke with a syrupy tone. "Oh, buddy. No need to worry about things like that. Leave that to me. We'll be able to take over any property we want." Steven's voice lowered, "Don't you understand? I can do whatever I want. Are you with us, or are you against us? Because from the way I see it, any man who turns his back on his country is a fucking traitor." Steven was nearly orgasmic with power, and Bryan knew he was trapped.

As Lauren stared at Steven pulling bread and mayonnaise from the refrigerator, she started to object. Bryan moved quickly to her and shushed her before

Steven noticed. Bryan loved Lauren in his own dysfunctional way, but his love was possessive. Lauren was his, not Steven's. He tried to put his arm on her waist, and Lauren shrank in on herself. Lauren did not want him touching her ever again. She felt like he must have known that she was done with him, and this was a trap. Steven glanced up to see her. "Well, hello there, princess. Nice that you could join us. So, here's the situation. And, if I say so myself, you should be so very honored. But I don't give a damn if you're not. Your home has been chosen as the new center of operations for the Defenders of the Homeland. You can call me Battalion Commander Jackson, and you can thank me now." Steven's lips curved menacingly.

Lauren stared blankly as if she hadn't heard. Bryan pretended excitement. "Isn't that great, babe? We're going to be part of taking our country back!" Steven glared at them both coldly.

"I don't understand. What do you mean?" Lauren's gray matter could not process his words.

Bryan jumped in nervously, still hoping to keep the situation under control. "You know, Uncle Sam needs us."

Lauren was shaking as the reality of what they were saying was steadily, painfully unfolding in her mind. She interrupted Bryan, stating firmly, "No way. This is my house. This land has been in my family for four generations. Steven, you need to leave now." She turned to Bryan for back up, but he stared at the floor with his arms folded over his chest.

Steven set down his sandwich and deliberately walked toward Lauren. Bryan watched as an expression of fear consumed her, yet she kept her feet firmly planted on the ground. Steven pulled back and slapped Lauren solidly in the face. Blood rushed from her nose and started pouring down her shirt. Her hands flew to her face as Steven pulled her to the floor by her hair where he kicked her firmly in the ribs. Bryan wanted to plug his ears to block her bellowing. He wanted to pull out his gun and shoot Steven between the eyes. Instead, he turned his head away so Steven wouldn't see his glassy eyes.

Lauren laid in a fetal position until Steven commanded, "Get this whore out of here. Bryan, lock her in the shed out back." Steven scoffed, "Next time I won't be so forgiving of back talk."

Lauren was still gasping for air as Bryan pulled her to her feet. He whispered, "Just shut your mouth, okay?"

He frog-marched her out the door, past the patch of daisies Lauren had seen the day before. They moved across the yard to the small outbuilding at the back of the property where Lauren kept rusting equipment she no longer used. The smell of engine oil flooded out as Bryan opened the door. Another storm was headed their way, and thunder rumbled in the distance. He shoved her inside, but Lauren caught the door before he could close it. "Bryan. Bryan…" she choked out. "You can't do this. There's no way. We can fix this still, right? What can we do? This can't be what you want!"

"It doesn't matter what I want. I'll come and get you after Steven settles down. Then you need to do what he says, okay? Don't challenge him. Treat him with respect. He's in charge around here now, and you've got to listen. Okay? You don't know what he's capable of."

Desperation rose in Lauren's voice, "No, I don't know what he's capable of. What have you gotten us into? Please, you owe it to me to tell me."

Bryan swallowed hard and looked over his shoulder to see if anyone could see them from the house windows. "I joined the militia last year, Lauren. We're… we're… going to clean things up. You'll see. Once we secure our people's existence, the world will be a better place. And now you're part of it, too. Steven's going to have the other wives meet with you tomorrow. They can help you with your clothes and knowing how to act. You don't have any idea what's best for you. Now, shut up, and let me get back."

"How are you protecting anyone with what you're doing? You're hurting people! You're hurting *me*!"

Bryan leapt at her and punched her in the stomach. Lauren doubled over and started coughing. "I told you to shut the fuck up. You're too stupid to understand. We're just defending ourselves. *They* want to replace us, Lauren. *They* started this, but we will end it."

Lauren gasped as Bryan slammed the door shut.

With Child

The stench of stale gas hung in the air like a thick blanket that covered everything, including Lauren's ability to think. After Bryan's assault, Lauren slid down the wall and stayed that way for a long time. The shed was dark and damp with just enough room for her to twine into a ball on the floor. Every part of her ached, and she was dying for a glass of water. And a cigarette. Lauren fantasized lighting her cigarette and putting the flame to the gas, bringing it all to an end. As Lauren nursed the image, she realized how close she was coming to her end. She couldn't do much more, and it terrified her. She'd been courting death with a lover's passion, but she didn't actually want to die. She just didn't know how to stop the hurt.

Lauren might have wanted to tune out all the horrors happening around her, but when it was at her doorstep, ignoring them was no longer a choice. Even with how ghastly Bryan had become, Lauren still could not have believed it could come to this. She figured she'd have to take a loyalty oath to the Defenders. She'd be pushed into a mold for one of their traditional wives, and any parts that didn't fit would be cut off and thrown away. Who would she be then? She'd be a cook. She'd be a housekeeper, and she would make babies, just as all the other wives. Babies were a subject that Lauren was spending a good deal of time trying not to think about. She rubbed her stomach where Bryan's punch landed. *What if...?*

Gales were tottering the shed and ripping at the boards. Lauren worried that the building would collapse. At least if she killed herself, she'd be in control of how her story ended, she thought. At that moment, she would not allow being trapped in that stinking hovel to be her last memory. As that understanding crystallized so too did another: she could not be a tradwife. Bryan claimed to be protecting her, but what was actually happening? She felt the opposite of being protected. Everything he said was a lie. They didn't want a white ethnostate to bring peace; they wanted to hurt and maim, and their theology was nothing more than a fig leaf for their rage. *I can't stay. I can't become one of them.*

Lauren felt as if the universe had opened a window of opportunity when a strong gust ripped off a chunk of the siding, exposing a large hole. Lauren could see debris flying by, and she realized how scared she was to go outside. She screamed as a large branch tore the hole even larger and mist began howling inside. This must be a tornado, she thought, as she searched through the hole. Several had torn through the area already that year. The winds were straight, but not as fierce as the derechos that ripped apart everything in their path often enough. Lauren rubbed her hands together. It was just a storm. She would be okay.

Her heart raced as she considered where she would go when Jack's words came to mind: *If you ever need anything...* She remembered where their farm was, and if she kept her head, she could get there. Surveying her options, Lauren concluded that if she could just get to the woods the trees would help break the wind and hide her as she escaped. Lauren mustered every ounce of courage within. She kicked hard at the remaining scraps of wood around the crater and eased out around the splinters. The wind was so powerful that it knocked her down and pain flared everywhere. Drenched and filthy, Lauren pushed herself to her feet. Lauren felt as if the energy of the storm was electrifying her soul, propelling her forward. Through force of will, she'd make it to Jack's house. She was not weak; she would survive.

Lauren ran as long and hard through the scrubby trees as she could. Mud caked to her shoes made her legs feel like weights. She only stopped momentarily to sip water gathered on leaves. She climbed a small hill that wasn't much more than a collection of rocks picked from the field. She scraped soil from her feet and tried to get her bearings. The water ran down her back, and her clothes were sopping wet. She was close. Hunger burned within her as she prayed to make it before she collapsed.

Lauren huffed and stumbled as she made it to Jack's road and climbed out from the overgrown ditch. The road was sloppy with ruts, and Lauren felt her ankle twist and a surge of pain. She ignored it as she limped to the house.

"Almost there," she said aloud, as aches emanated from every cell of her body. She hadn't noticed the lightning crackling around her and her arm hair standing on end as an immense purple flash threw her onto her back. Lauren hit her head sharply and sprawled out motionless on the grass as another round of torrential rain started.

A little girl with red polka-dot boots, a bouncing ponytail, and a spirit more adventurous than her parents wished came out to inspect the damage from the storm. She yelled and dropped her basket when she saw Lauren lying there bleeding from the head. She ran back to the house, toot sweet.

"There's a strange lady in the yard, and she's hurt bad."

Jack and his wife Rosa exchanged concerned glances then without a word, Rosa grabbed her medical bag and rushed outside. Jack was fast behind her and gasped.

"That's Dale's girl! What on earth?"

Rosa and Jack each draped one of her arms around their necks and gingerly got her to the house and laid her down on the bed in the hallway alcove.

Rosa lamented, "Looks like she had more trouble than the lightning. She's bruised and battered all over. Gloria, Jack, get my supplies. I'll get her cleaned up, then we'll just have to wait."

And wait they did. Rosa cleaned her dressings, fed her ice chips, read her poems, and talked to her for three days while searching for signs of recovery. Lauren was healing, but when she finally opened her eyes, she could not remember a thing about how she'd gotten there. No one was around as she tried to focus her eyes. She felt as thin and fragile as a piece of gauze. *Bryan?* She called out. Rosa heard from the kitchen and came to her.

"Hi there. I'm Rosa. There is no Bryan here. We found you, and you were very hurt. Do you know how you got here?"

Lauren shook her head as memories began bubbling in. Still, she couldn't put it all together just yet. But the feelings were all there.

"My husband Jack and I knew your father. We think that's why you must have come. It looks like you were running from something. From Bryan?"

Lauren shut her eyes tight and hot tears leaked out around them. She said nothing.

Rosa sighed, "Okay, I can see you're still trying to get your bearings. You gave us a real scare, you know! I'll send Gloria in with some tea and broth, that'll help get your strength back. We can talk later."

Lauren turned her head and wept into the sheets. She remembered why she was there and felt awful for bringing the threat of the Defenders. *I should never have come. They don't deserve this.*

Rosa brought Jack in to try. "Hello, Lauren? Do you remember me? I'm Jack Fitzpatrick. We met at the store."

Lauren wanted to respond. But when she opened her soft lips, no words came.

The family left Lauren to her misery, but Rosa routinely checked in. She'd been a nurse at the Clinic back in the day and studied alternative healing. Her skills had come in handy with the breakdown of traditional medical systems. On the third occasion Rosa popped in, Lauren had found her voice.

"I'm sorry I didn't answer before. I was overwhelmed, and I'm putting you in danger. I feel so guilty. I shouldn't have come. If you tell me where my things are, I'll be on my way."

Rosa perched on the white stool adjacent to the bed and folded her hands in her lap. "Now, hold up. Why don't you stay a minute, and tell me about it? Maybe we can help."

Lauren sniffed. "It's not that I want to leave. It's just not fair to your family. I wasn't thinking. I was just scared and remembered that Jack told me to reach out if I needed anything. I don't think this is what he had in mind."

She took a deep breath and told Rosa about Bryan and the Defenders.

"I could tell that all your injuries weren't caused by that lightning. You're pretty beaten up. There's something else, too. I wasn't sure, but when I was taking care of you, I suspected that you were with child. I did a pregnancy test, and it came back positive. I didn't mean to violate your privacy, but I had to know all what was going on so I could take care of you."

The blood drained from Lauren's face. Her suspicions had been correct.

"Are you sure? I miss my period all the time."

"Yes, I'm sure. I did two tests."

"Shit... I don't even know what to think. I don't want this, and I feel like I have to tell Bryan. It's his child."

"Honey, I'm not sure that's a good idea. Women are at so much greater risk of being murdered by their abuser when they're pregnant or have a new baby. You're not safe with him."

Abuser? Lauren hadn't thought of him that way before. Did that make her a victim. She shuddered. "Safe? I don't even know what that feels like anymore."

Rosa smoothed Lauren's hair. "You will know it one day. I can sense it."

"So, you can see the future?" Lauren was skeptical.

"No... not exactly. But I feel things."

Lauren thought of everything she'd been working through lately. "Yeah, me too. But I don't feel anything right now, except that I don't want to be pregnant." Lauren felt the world collapsing in around her.

"You don't have to be, if you don't want this baby. There are options."

Lauren looked at Rosa with fear and confusion, "Abortion is illegal."

"Women have been ending unwanted pregnancies for thousands of years. I have herbs."

"I'm not sure. I'm really confused." Lauren couldn't process what Rosa was offering.

"Thinking of bringing a new life into this world is not an easy decision, especially with the world as it is now. In the end, it's your body and you need to be the one making the decision. You're the one who has to live with it, so you should have the choice."

Lauren stared into nothing. "*My* body? Huh? I just don't feel like I have the right to do what I want or to say what I want for myself."

"No one has more of a right than you, Lauren. Why would you say that?"

Lauren swallowed hard and fought back tears. "Because no one cares what I think. My opinions don't matter. *I* don't fucking matter."

"That's not true. You matter, Lauren." Rosa soothed.

"No, I don't. I never have. So, I just try to push who I am all the way down and away."

Shame and grief roiled around in Lauren's chest. She'd never before said these things aloud and couldn't believe the words that were coming out of her mouth. She heard Bryan's admonitions in her head, You're weak. You're pathetic.

Rosa was firm, but kind. "If we don't deal with our big feelings, they will deal with us. That's for sure. And honey, you are important. Everyone is, just by virtue of existing in this world. You don't need to do anything or prove your value. You're worthwhile because you are."

"Well, that's not the message the world has sent me. In fact, it's told me again and again what I want and need isn't important."

"I wonder if it's the world telling you that, or you're telling yourself that?" Lauren didn't answer. "Here's what I know. Your dad adored you. He always said that you were a sensitive person in a world of callous fools. I think you've been worn down, honey. You're just plum wore out by everything that's happened. You lost yourself along the way, and it'll take time. Be gentle with yourself."

"I am tired. So, so tired. I feel like I could sleep a hundred years. Aside from Bryan, I've also been having these strange attacks, or episodes, where I'm overwhelmed with all this stuff, my own feelings, those of other people, everything. It just floods in, and I can't stop it."

Rosa smiled a little. "You're coming into your own, is all. Your mind won't let you shut it all out anymore. It wants to be free. You have to let yourself feel things again, Lauren. There's no other way."

Lauren didn't want to listen to Rosa anymore. She didn't know if her mind wanted to be free, but she wanted to be free from Rosa at that moment. Lauren believed that she knew the truth about herself. Rosa didn't know how broken she was. Lauren kept trying to imagine herself with a baby, and she knew she didn't have the strength to care for a child on her own. *Maybe I should go back to Bryan? He is the child's father, and don't children need their fathers?* More of his accusations came to her: *You're impossible to love. You're a selfish child.* How could she be responsible for another life when she couldn't even handle her own? Lauren felt as if she was drowning.

As daylight broke through the small window at the end of the hall, it brought clarity. Lauren could smell pancakes cooking and called to the kitchen. She was still too weak to get up. "Rosa!"

Rosa walked into the hall wiping her plump hands on her stiff brown apron. "What you need?"

"Nothing. I just wanted to tell you something. I guess I still don't know what I want. But I know what I don't want. This child cannot be raised by such hate-filled people. Bryan says he's doing this to defend white children, but all I see is them tearing everyone down."

Rosa squeezed her, and it made Lauren stiffen. She wasn't used to being touched. "I'm glad. We were so worried about you. I know it's hard to leave someone like Bryan."

"*Why* is it hard, though? I don't understand what I was thinking. Why part of me still wants him?" Lauren felt like a fool.

"You weren't thinking clearly. You couldn't. People like that know how to divert your mind and heart. They rip apart who you are, so they can rebuild you in their image. That's what Bryan would do if you went back. You would lose yourself completely."

"I feel like I already did." Lauren said sadly.

"You'll find her again, Lauren. She's still there."

In Our Bones

Three Words

Over the next few weeks, Lauren's strength returned as her bruises healed. She became close to the family and began finding moments of unexpected joy. Watching the Fitzpatrick family together reminded Lauren of how much she'd lost, but also how much she had never had. Lauren's mother hadn't been one to display affection openly, but Rosa smothered her children with love. Lauren would sometimes look away, embarrassed. She realized that some of what was blocking her likely went back much farther back than she'd realized.

Rosa's love for her kids made Lauren think that hope was possible in this dark world. It almost made her think that maybe she could raise a child herself, but she kept Rosa's bundle of herbs tucked away in her alcove. Sometimes she'd take out the package and delicately press them to her. Sometimes it was the only thing that quelled her panic. Lauren's belly was swelling, but her heart wasn't. She could not connect with the life growing inside of her, and it made her desperate. It confirmed her worst fear, that she that was defective – not sufficiently womanly or maternal. Whenever Lauren tried to decide what to do about the baby, she'd fall back into her old shoddy coping mechanism. Lauren would shut down. She cried frequently and was prone to bouts of lying in bed. Gloria would worry and ask, "What's wrong with her?" The question was bigger than one for which Rosa had answers. She would simply say, "She's hurting and needs time."

Gloria sat with Lauren frequently and read to her from a book of sunny poetry. Lauren gained a deep affection for the girl and would brush and braid her hair. Eventually, Gloria's hugs were something Lauren asked for and sunk into. Rosa also talked to Lauren about ways to manage her feelings, something so basic Lauren was flustered to have never learned them before – like taking deep breaths and mindfulness to remain present when she was stressed. Jack reminded Lauren of her father, and she remembered that there were men were nothing like Bryan and Steven. Lauren took to bed less frequently over time, and her tears weren't as intense. She wanted to believe that Rosa was right about her having a future.

Lauren avoided thinking of next steps. But one evening as the family played cards, Jack inquired, "Lauren, we are happy to have you here with us. But I know you've got a sister. You haven't had us call her or anything. I was just wondering why?"

Lauren colored. "Yeah, she's got a little boy, too. I miss him. Rachel and I just don't have a good relationship. I've been afraid to tell her what's going on."

Rosa said, "She's family. I think you need to give her a chance."

"I suppose, yes. I should. Can I call her?"

It took Lauren a few more days to muster the courage. Her stomach gripped as the phone rang.

"Hello."

"Hi, Rachel. It's Lauren."

"Wow. It's been so long. I'm really surprised you called." Her voice was annoyed, but only a little.

Lauren pushed on. "I know. I'm sorry I cut you out of my life. It was just too complicated." Lauren was trying to stay calm, but blurted out, "Bryan was abusing me, and I'm pregnant."

Rachel stayed silent for many moments, while Lauren fought the urge to hang up. Rachel choked out, "Okay. Okay. Where are you now? We'll figure this out."

By the time they'd finished talking, Lauren was suspicious that she'd judged Rachel as harshly as she'd felt judged. But she remained somewhat worried as she hadn't told Rachel the whole story about the militia. Still, she told Rosa, "It's time for me to be with my family." When Rosa hugged her and told her how happy she was for her, Lauren felt a gush of love and hugged her back. It had been so long since she'd experienced such a sensation that it made her cry again – this time, they were tears of bliss.

On Lauren's last night with the Fitzpatricks, she forced herself to think of the child within her. Lauren believed that if she could feel a spark of love, she would be okay. But the more she concentrated, the emptier she became. Rosa told her that it was probably just stress, and that she needed to relax. A decision would come when it was ready. Lauren wished that she had an ounce of Rosa's tranquility. Lauren held the bag of dried plants and thought of their power to end one life and restore another. Her eyes closed, and she found herself standing in a vast field. Across the way, a little girl sat on a rock, picking petals off a daisy. Lauren approached and the girl smiled. "Hi," she said.

Lauren knelt. She knew this was her child and reached out to touch her. The girl said, "Don't. I'm not staying. I just wanted you to know that you're going to be alright." The girl stood and said, "It's your time now." Lauren watched as the girl walked away in her shimmering dress, dropping petals as she went. Lauren tried to run after her but stopped as the girl faded away.

Lauren woke up in a pool of sweat and blood.

Jack came to wake her and saw the red. He rushed to get his wife, and Rosa confirmed that Lauren had lost the baby. "How do you feel?"

Before she could think, Lauren replied, "Free."

She didn't tell Rosa about the dream because part of her felt that she'd killed the child. She harbored guilt that she couldn't define. As she was preparing to leave, Lauren looked around and took in the shelves surrounding the little bed she'd called home. She wanted to remember every inch of it, since she'd emerged from more than one coma while lying there. She packed a picture that Gloria had drawn and put her shoes back on, now liberated from their mud sheath. Lauren wasn't ready to go, but she was as ready as she could be to see her family again. Rosa gave Lauren an embroidered cotton scarf to protect her wound, with delicate flowers adorning the edge. Lauren was tying it on and admiring Rosa's handiwork when she saw herself in the mirror. Her eyes weren't happy, but they weren't sad.

Jack decided that for cover they'd transport a load of straw to town along with some chickens. Lauren would ball in the middle of the bales so no one would see her. The family gathered in the driveway in the shadow of the scorched maple. As they were ready for her to climb in the truck, Lauren couldn't stop the sentiments overtaking her. She would miss them so much.

"I can never repay what you did for me."

Rosa teared up and grinned. "Don't worry, honey. You're going to pay it forward. Your journey is just beginning."

"I don't know why you think so much of me."

"Because I see the greatness that you can't yet."

Lauren just shook her head. *Yeah, right.*

Gloria wrapped her arms tight around Lauren. "I love you," she said.

Lauren hadn't heard those words since her dad was still alive. Bryan never said them. Lauren steadied herself and said back those three words that had the capacity to change the world. She embarrassed herself, though as the words felt foreign in her mouth. She gave Gloria a quick kiss on the head before she climbed inside the truck.

Lauren was hot and sticky as she bounced around in the back. Her stomach and back were tightly cramped as the blood continued to flow. She wondered if the child had known that she was feeble, wondered if she'd been rejected again. Then she remembered the words from the girl from the dream: *It's your time now.* Lauren didn't believe that this dream was real, but it seemed so much that she wanted to believe. The whole time to Rachel's house, Lauren repeated in her head: *It's my time now.* She prayed for this to be true.

Sooner than Lauren thought they backed into the driveway of the two-story stucco house where Rachel and Ben were living. Jack approached the door with a chicken under his arm, indicating to anyone who might be peering out the window a plausible reason for the visit. Chickens and other livestock were ubiquitous even in the cities by then. When Jack got back to the truck, they unloaded the straw into the garage, and Lauren slipped in and moved to hide in the back. She stuffed herself behind a cabinet as she heard them pull away.

Goodbye. Thank you. Surprising herself, she wished she could give them a long hug.

As Lauren waited in the cool quiet of the garage, she held onto the concern that Rachel would make her leave once she found out the whole story. After years of shoving unpleasant thoughts away, Lauren could not stop worrying. She slumped onto the floor and folded in on herself. With each sound, she'd freeze, imagining Bryan at the door. When Lauren heard the garage door actually open, her heart pounded, and she recoiled. The garage was silent as Rachel entered. She called out, "Lauren?"

At the sound of Rachel's voice, Lauren bolted up.

"I'm here. Oh God, Rachel, I was afraid you weren't coming! I mean, I knew you would. But I was so scared."

Lauren started sobbing hard. She wanted to embrace Rachel but remembered that their family didn't do that. She'd grown more accustomed to the Fitzpatrick's than she'd even realized until then.

"Of course, I was coming. I could never leave you. Why would you think that?"

"Maybe because there's so much I haven't told you." Lauren tried to breathe like Rosa had taught her.

"There's more?"

"A lot more." Lauren began with, "I didn't know at first what he was doing. But then I didn't know how to get away."

"What was he doing?" Rachel's voice was nearing a shriek.

"Bryan's with the Defenders of the Homeland, Rachel. I swear I didn't know…" Lauren dissolved, while Rachel folded her arms across her chest and huffed.

"I believe you, but that's really freaking scary, Laur. Does he know about the baby? And does he know where I live? I've been seeing their cars going past the house, but not any more than usual. I don't want to leave Ben by himself any longer. I'm glad you told me, but I'm terrified for all of us. If Bryan finds out about Ben, and you know his paperwork is forged…"

"I know. I'm such a fucking idiot." Lauren felt herself shrinking back into that same hurt little girl she used to be. She fought to keep herself together. She couldn't tell Rachel about the baby, not yet at least.

"You're not an idiot. But this is really bad. My guess is with how you said the commander was treating Bryan, they're not making finding you a priority. He's got your house; he doesn't need you." At the word *house* Lauren whimpered. Rachel continued, "Your disappearance will be another way to humiliate Bryan. That's the way these guys think. Even so, I don't want anyone turning you in, so come to the back door once it's completely dark outside. We can't be too careful. I guess it's time to pull the trigger on my plan."

In Our Bones

Peeling Away

Rachel had seen the writing on the wall for some time. She began researching, planning, and stocking supplies for a day like today. She'd assumed that Lauren was a lost cause but leaving their mother behind was more than she could bear. She'd been trying to hang on until Ann passed, but fate and Lauren's choices had tipped her hand. Rachel pulled out her stack of papers and got to work finalizing what to do next.

Ben sat on his bed watching a show, happily unaware that his world was about to be turned upside down. He wandered into the kitchen and saw Rachel surrounded by lists and maps. He had the dazed look of someone who'd done nothing but stare at screens for hours. He rubbed his eyes.

"Mom, what's for dinner? I'm hungry."

The sun was low in the sky and painted oranges and yellows across the horizon.

"I'm not sure yet, but let me grab you a snack, and then we need to talk." Ben tensed up, and Rachel could sense his worry. "You're not in trouble. We just need to go over a few things." She put a small plain muffin on the table and invited him to sit down.

"Can I at least have some honey with it?" Ben begged.

Rachel hesitated by instinct, then remembered that she'd be leaving it all behind soon. She knew that he hated so much blandness. "Yes, you may. Do you want a little raspberry jam, too?" Ben's eyes lit up.

Rachel sat down with dread at what she needed to tell her little boy, peeling away yet another layer of what had become normal life. He deserved so much better than what that the world had given him. "You remember that I told you that I had a sister, right? Lauren. You knew her when you were little, but we haven't seen her in a long time."

"I don't remember her."

Rachel winced. "Well, she loved you. But then she ended up with a bad man, someone like the ones who made it so you couldn't go to school. This man wants her to be his girlfriend, but she doesn't want that anymore. So, she's not safe with him, and she's coming here tonight."

"What if they come here looking for her? I'm scared."

"I know. So am I, but she's our family." Rachel was angry with Lauren for frightening her son.

"She's not my family. She's your family."

"Ben, that's not nice. You're my family, and so is she."

Ben stomped around the room. "I don't want any more bad people around. It's not fair!"

"No, it's not fair. But it is what it is. Now, go. I have a lot of work to do."

Rachel was frustrated with herself for not being more understanding. She wondered if she should be helping Lauren after all, but also believed that she had little choice. She couldn't just abandon her. Rachel cleaned up the papers on the table and went to start their dinner. There would be no skimping on her meal tonight. Rachel had a decent amount of food stored up but was as conscious as an accountant of every calorie they consumed. She couldn't get the image out of her head of the poor starving children with their mothers she'd sometimes seen during pledge drives on television, way back when. They had seemed so far away and disconnected from her reality at the time. Now she imagined all too easily the pain that those mothers must have endured cradling their emaciated babies.

Lauren laid down on the cold concrete floor of the garage and tried to rest. Mercifully, the night crept in and she lurched up the backstairs of the deck and knocked at the door, shaking with anxiety. Rachel rushed to let her in. Ben heard the knock and stood at the doorway to the kitchen. He glared at her.

"Ben, this is your Aunt Lauren."

A ripple of mortification shot through her when she realized her own nephew didn't know her anymore. She couldn't come to terms with having prioritized someone like Bryan over her family.

"Hi Ben. We used to know each other. I hope we can be friends again."

Ben shrugged, "I don't want to be friends with anyone who brings bad people here."

"I'm so sorry. I won't let anything happen to you. I promise." Lauren teared up again.

"You can't keep that promise. No one can keep anything terrible from happening!" Ben ran out of the room blubbering.

Lauren turned to Rachel. "I'm sorry. He hates me."

"He doesn't hate you. He's just afraid. We need to eat first, then we can talk about what to do. Okay?"

Their evening meal was uncomfortable and quiet as Ben sulked, and neither sister could think of anything to talk about that was appropriate in front of him. Rachel hurried him to bed, so they could go over her plans. They settled on the couch.

"I want to get as far away from Bryan and these so-called Defenders as we can," Rachel said.

"I know, I guess. I just really hadn't thought about anything much beyond getting here. It was like I had tunnel vision." Lauren felt a headache coming on.

"I'm sure it's been tough. But it's time that we faced reality about what our country has become." Lauren looked down, bracing for the rest of Rachel's lecture. "I'm sure you don't want to hear this, but I just need to lay a few things out. I'm not trying to be mean, because I know everything with Bryan was overwhelming. But there have been a lot of terrible things happening to a lot of people for a long time. And I don't think that you have been willing to see that. I need you to understand that Ben is not safe here, and your actions have made it worse. I want you to be okay, but this isn't just about you anymore." Rachel hadn't meant to come across as so angry but couldn't stop herself. It kept coming. "Dad and I tried to warn you. But you didn't want to listen. Now these crazy people in power just do whatever the heck they want to do!" She let out a long breath and evened her temper. "So, I've been tuning into these Resistance Radio broadcasts and working on a strategy to get out of the country."

Lauren didn't know how to take what Rachel was throwing at her. She was so used to being criticized by Bryan that humiliation was overtaking her.

"I'm sorry, Rach. I know that I've made a lot of bad decisions. I'm so sorry." She laid her head down on the sofa's armrest. This was the side of Rachel that Lauren had been expecting all along.

"I'll head over to the nursing home and get Mom tomorrow. They haven't been answering their phone…"

Lauren's thoughts raced. "How are we supposed to be running away from here with a little boy and a sick old woman in tow? That's crazy!"

"I don't know how it'll work either, but you've given us no choice." Rachel had a hard edge to her voice. "But Mom won't last long, and I want her with us at the end. When I was there before, the sheets had obviously not been changed in who knows how long and her hair was all matted. The place is falling apart, Lauren. I've been planning to bring her home with me, regardless. But I knew how hard it would be and been trying to get things ready. I guess I have to be ready now."

Lauren felt humiliated at Rachel's admonition. Lauren hadn't been to see their mother in months. Guilt was consuming her. She muttered, "I shouldn't have come here."

Rachel's voice softened. "Don't say that. I'm glad you came. We can't change what is done, but we can learn from it. The most important thing right now is that we get away from here. Many years ago, I heard of this place called Nacia in Kanata. It's a city designed intentionally to withstand just about anything, from fires to food shortages. I haven't heard anything about it for almost ten years, so I'm not certain that they're still there, or if they're taking in new people or anything. But that's the safest place I can think of for Ben."

Years before, the Canadian Supreme Court ruled that the country had been illegally taken from its native inhabitants. Canada's tribal governments worked together with the existing government to decide how to move forward. The country remained a democracy and was similar to before. However, a number of changes were made to the Constitution to respect tribal sovereignty, and tribal leadership decided to change the country's name to the native version of the word Canada. Thus, America's neighbor to the north became known thereafter as Kanata.

Lauren was puzzled. "I thought they closed their border to American refugees?"

"They did. But there are coyotes that will help us cross. We have to at least try to get there. Ben needs to be somewhere that he has a chance to grow up. Somewhere he has a chance to grow old." Rachel was near hysteria, "He has no life here! No future. He's miserable. I'm miserable. It's long past time to go. I know I sound upset with you, but in reality, it's a blessing. I've been so ready to go for so long."

Lauren eased inside. It was nice to not be blamed anymore. "I don't really trust myself with any decisions right now. But I trust you. So, let's do it. Just getting the fuck out of this town would be nice." Lauren saw Rachel wince at her swearing. *Some things don't change.*

Lauren asked more questions about Nacia and was starting to believe that it could be everything Rachel said it was. Still she thought of herself as someone undeserving of an opinion. Besides, she did want Ben to have a better life. She could remember the first time she held him. He was so tiny and frail. When he'd joined their family as a baby, Rachel had been sketchy on the details of how he came and why. Piecing it together in her mind now, Lauren guessed that Rachel hadn't trusted her to know. Waves of shame washed over her as she realized how selfish she'd been for so long. Lauren was exhausted and splintering.

She laid her head down and asked, "Can you tell me the story of Ben coming to you? The real story. It feels important for me to know."

Rachel's mouth puckered, and she looked uncertain. "Okay, I'll tell you. But no one else can know. This is for family only."

Benjamin had been left alone crying for hours. His mom overdosed alone on one of the many synthetic opioids that were going around. When the cops arrived, the smell of her corpse already filled the dank cluttered room. The older cop, Officer Doyle, bent down and picked up the mewling listless boy from his crib. He looked at the mother. She had been beautiful, he thought. She had vacant pale eyes and soft curled hair. She laid on the bed next to a pool of vomit. Doyle imagined the baby looked like his nephew did when he was born, with dark straight hair and light brown skin.

He and the other responding officer poked around the room and there was no birth certificate or proof of citizenship. Since they had no way to contact next of kin and the child was obviously not white, Doyle knew the feds would consider him an *illegal*. He was supposed to call the Department of Children and Families to take him into custody. But Doyle couldn't. He'd heard about what was happening to the kids, and he couldn't be part of it. The officer joined the force decades before because he had wanted to help people. Now he was stuck with bullshit like this and some punk for a partner who he figured would sell his own grandma for a few bucks.

Doyle stuffed a wad of bills in his partner's hand dismissively. "I'm going to handle this one. Can you see if you can find some milk or something?" There were a few baby things strewn about the small dismal room.

Doyle made calls until he finally reached one of the last remaining social workers who still had a job with the county. After the economy collapsed, the federal government gradually quit funding anything they couldn't control, which included state and local governments. When Party insiders declared they wanted to shrink government down to the size that it could be drowned in a bathtub, few had paid attention. Now, they had come close.

The other cop scrounged around for powdered formula and made up a bottle, just like he'd done when his sister was born. What Doyle didn't know about him was that he didn't want to take bribes. But when his pay got cut so much that he couldn't pay the bills anymore, he had no choice. He was supporting his whole family with one measly paycheck. When given few options, the line between right and wrong became so thin that many couldn't see it anymore.

They waited for what felt like an eternity and were beginning to wonder if the social worker had turned them into the feds or the militia when she finally arrived. The worker fed the dead woman's child until his eyes fell closed, and she whispered to the woman, "Your baby will be okay. I'll make sure of it. I know just the person to ask." She switched into baby talk and stroked Ben's forehead. "Yes, I do know someone for you. Yes, I do."

The President had created the Department of Children and Families for the alleged purpose of saving the many orphaned children who were suffering. But the executive order was really intended to frighten people and fill the big privately-owned warehouse detention facilities that were built by the President's friends and donors. DCF would take any non-white looking kids it could round up, regardless of their actual citizenship status, and hand them over to them to central processing facilities. From there the kids ended up indefinitely in warehouse prisons, unless they were lucky enough that the right bribe got into the right hands to buy their freedom. A good many were also dumped alone on the streets of some poor country America bullied into taking them. The "suitable" ones were taken to homes where they were promised an education and a good life as missionaries. They'd learn the gospel and spread it across the land to earn their keep. Some people took in these children and cared for them. But that wasn't the fate met by most, unless you can call scrubbing floors and sucking old men's cocks spreading the Good Word.

Rachel had been friends with the social worker for years. They'd gone to a few protests together and wrote postcards to politicians and such back in the days before that became illegal. The worker showed up at Rachel's door unannounced. The baby was so teensy, so adorable, and so vulnerable that Rachel could not say no. She had never imagined that she would become a mom at her age and had been okay with that. Cuddling that sleepy baby made her wonder how she could live another moment without him, though. Her eyes filled as she said, "I'm going to name him Benjamin."

The social worker knew someone who could forge a new birth certificate, and just like that he would become

Rachel's son. Before she left, the social worker pressed a small fraying picture into Rachel's hands.

"Keep this. He'll want it someday."

Bobby Pins

The house was silent, but Lauren's head was a torrent of screams. Sleep eluded her as she tried to build her courage for the journey ahead. She kept her tears at bay, as anger with herself was papering over the sadness. The chronicle of Ben's adoption from the night before was seared in her mind. Lauren finally fully understood the gravity of her choices. She thought back to a time before the President's second election when Rachel had gotten herself worked-up about the child detentions at the border.

They were at their folks' house for supper. Lauren kept saying, "Their parents shouldn't have brought them here. It's their fault if the kids suffer. Not my problem."

Lauren could still see the disgust on Rachel's face. At the time, Lauren believed that her sister was over-reacting.

Rachel slammed her glass down, "You're trying not to take sides in a world where morality demands it, Lauren. Can't you see what the President is doing to this country? Why won't you do anything?"

Lauren answered, "Because I am only responsible for myself, Rachel. These other people need to take responsibility for their own lives."

Looking back, the truth was that Lauren could not stand to see the pictures of the children detained at the border. She couldn't hear the stories of what they'd gone through, were going through and that the government was about to put them through. As with so many things, it wasn't that Lauren didn't care; she cared too much and was overwhelmed with the situation. Tuning it out and blaming the parents was vastly easier than coming to terms with what was happening. Now she was mortified with herself. No wonder Rachel was angry.

Lauren heard the door creak open, as if someone was sneaking. A bolt of fear coursed through her as she popped up, ready for Bryan. Ready for a fight. What she saw was a heavy-hearted little boy staring at her.

"Ben, you scared me so much. Do you need something?"

"No. I was just hoping you were gone."

He turned and left without another word.

The look in his eyes had been eviscerating. Lauren felt her mind start spinning into the emotional chaos of another episode. Rosa had helped her understand that she was powerless to stop it, but she could learn to control it. At this moment, there was no control. There was no stopping the ache, but Lauren was less scared than she'd been. She knew that feelings wouldn't break her. Rosa had said, "Your tears are how you rebuild yourself, Lauren. Let the feelings out. Let them come because their job is to flush out the agony, you're holding in. You will never heal if you keep it inside." Lauren let herself cry until her pillow was damp, and her torture eased.

Rachel heard Lauren but was busy preparing for their departure and wanted to give her space. When there were no more sobs coming from the room, Rachel went to sit with her. The curtains were drawn tight and the room had the faint smell of lemon oil furniture polish. Rachel asked gently, "Is there anything I can do?"

Lauren stayed turned away; she couldn't face her. "No. I just need a minute."

"Jack told me about the baby."

Lauren stayed still. "Oh. I meant to say something. It's just been a lot." Lauren had yet to feel anything more about the loss of the baby than vague sense of responsibility for the death. She didn't want to tell Rachel that.

"Is that why you're crying?" Rachel ventured.

"I suppose, yes. But there's so much more. I feel so guilty. Ben came in and said he wished I was gone."

"He'll come around. I think he's just overloaded. I talked to him about the plan. He was pretty upset, and I think he blames you. I tried to explain, but it'll take time for him to understand."

"He's right, though. I've been... what do they call it? Complicit? I let all this happen. Maybe if I had done more…"

"I know you feel guilty. I said a lot of things last night about your lack of engagement, but I hope you also realize that the problems were bigger than any one of us could solve alone. Of *course,* you should have done more. All of us should have."

"But I did nothing. I literally ignored everything you and Dad told me. I even said that I didn't care if the President was racist because he'd fix the economy. What the fuck was I thinking? I joked about the climate, saying stupid crap like on cold days we could use a little more warming. Everything you said would happen has come true, and I should have listened. I should have done something."

"The world isn't on fire because of you. You're here now, and we're going to face this together like a family."

Lauren felt a little better afterward and forced herself to get up and get moving. *Was culpability a reason to not work?* No. There was much to do. In the living room, Lauren watched as Rachel slammed down her cell phone in frustration.

Rachel grumped, "They're still not answering. We just need to get her and go."

"I agree. Let's get everything packed first, though? That way we can just leave town right away. I think Mom will get more disoriented if we bring her here first. I'm so worried about all this, still."

Rachel's voice was condescending. "Well, you got any other ideas?"

"No, of course not. I was just saying." Lauren's feelings were hurt, and she was so very tired of being hurt.

Rachel didn't notice. "Can you get those boxes of dehydrated food and look for the one with the wind-up flashlights and ham radios."

Lauren went downstairs to Rachel's basement and combed through her extensive collection of prepper items. Rachel had more than they could possibly take, and Lauren imagined Rachel stress buying whatever she saw advertised online in the years building up to the collapse. Lauren worked from Rachel's list to assemble coherent boxes and started bringing things upstairs.

Rachel was in Ben's room with him helping him pack. Going through his things was excruciating, since each item was a memory that he wanted to hold onto. He was bargaining to keep everything, of course, and Rachel knew that they could keep almost nothing. They finally agreed that he could fill a bag with whatever was his most special stuff and they would come back for the rest one day if they could. She did not want a power struggle on top of everything else, but she hated lying to him. Rachel knew they would never be back. She also knew that it was doubtful that that broken Batman figurine was really one of his favorite things. At a time when his life was spinning out of his control, she figured it was best to give him as much discretion as she could reasonably give. If that meant a broken Batman, so be it. As they were finishing up, Ben clasped the photo of him as an infant. It looked like it had been taken in one of those little photo booths. Ben's mother was holding him on her lap smiling. The picture invariably made Rachel feel downcast, because the woman looked so happy and would be dead so soon after it was taken. Ben kissed the picture. "We need to bring her, too."

Rachel had him watch a show to keep him out of the way and was moving onto the next thing when she got a ping on her phone. She gasped. "No! Checkpoints!" She darted downstairs to find Lauren, near hysterics.

Lauren had never seen Rachel look so alarmed, and it terrified her. Rachel was the one in control, the one to lead the way. Lauren was certain that they'd be lost if it weren't for her.

"What's going on? You're scaring me."

Rachel shoved her phone at Lauren and said, "Read it for yourself."

By order of the President: All travel between cities has been suspended. Only official government business is permitted until further notice. Enforcement checkpoints will be in place. Anyone without appropriate paperwork will be subject to arrest.

Rachel started pacing the room. "Why are they doing this?" She burst into tears. "We waited too long!"

Lauren struggled for calm. "We'll figure it out. It's going to be okay."

Rachel started yelling, "How? How are we going to figure this out, Lauren?"

"I don't know, okay. But we will. We just have to keep our heads. And we've got to hold on to hope that we'll make it, Rachel. Because if we don't have hope what else do we have?" The more Rachel panicked; the calmer Lauren became. She realized that her family needed her to be level.

"Yeah. Whatever. You're the goddess of hope now, I guess?"

Lauren winced. "I know you're angry, but I don't deserve that. I'm just trying to help. Yes, this is a disaster, and I'm worried, too. But we will figure it out!"

Lauren stood dumbfounded as Rachel stormed out of the room and slammed her bedroom door.

Ben heard the commotion and came to check. Lauren saw him in his bedroom doorway and called out to him.

"It's okay, sweetie. Your mom's just upset, but everything will be alright."

As she spoke, Lauren realized that her sister's reaction was fueled by her worry about Ben. Lauren felt immature for not having understood the pressure her sister was under. Ben went back into his room and shut the door. Lauren wondered if he would ever forgive her. She wondered if she'd ever forgive herself.

Lauren kept packing, hoping Rachel would find a solution. She was bullish when Rachel shouted, "Can you come?"

Lauren stepped inside the mauve bedroom to see Rachel sprawled out on a puffy bedspread.

"Have you come up with something?" Lauren asked.

"No. Nothing. I just wanted some company before the Gestapo came for us." Her voice was devoid of emotion, which alarmed Lauren more than Rachel's shouting.

"Stop that. We'll think of something. What about back roads?"

"I don't think that's safe, either. They've got drones and patrols everywhere. We can't run, and we can't hide forever."

Lauren's gaze fell across the room at her sister's decor. Lauren hadn't been in this room for so long, she hadn't remembered how frilly Rachel's taste was. The room looked like that of an elderly lady, and Lauren remembered the nearly twenty-year gap in their ages.

Her sister looked feeble, lying with her long salt and pepper hair covering her face. Lauren fought for what to say next when the closet caught her attention.

Lauren's expression turned to elation as she walked over and pulled out two long dresses. "Rachel, we can hide in plain sight. Right under their fucking noses!"

"Don't swear so much. I don't like it. What are you talking about?"

"Don't you see! These dresses! So many of the women and tradwives dress like this in their movement. We can, too, and they'll think we're one of them."

Rachel peeked over to see the dresses she'd worn for a community theater production of O'Pioneers during what felt like another lifetime ago. "Huh," was all she said, but the gears of her mind were working. "Just because we're dressed like them doesn't mean we have a reason to be out. You saw the text. Official business only."

"You were telling me about the kids they're sending off to work as missionaries. What if we say that we're taking Ben to a church for service? That would be official business." Lauren was proud of herself for coming up with such a plan so quickly, though she was sure Rachel would reject it.

Rachel stayed quiet for a long time. Lauren's confidence was plummeting until Rachel said, "I actually think that could work. I could print off a letter for us to bring. I bought a forged government seal a long time ago. At the time I wasn't sure why, but it seems that this might be just the reason. Lauren, you're a genius!"

Lauren beamed; this was the first time she could recall Rachel seeming proud of her. Her joy was quickly replaced with brooding. If they went with her plan and it failed, it would be her fault. "What if we get caught?"

"There's a reason they put out that alert. Something big is coming, I know it. This is the best shot we've got. It's only a matter of time before they find you, and Ben and I will be caught up with whatever happens."

"I'm sorry."

"That's not my point. Stop pouting. We have to go. We can have Ben say that he only speaks Mixtec, so he doesn't get questioned. I hope no one we deal with was a missionary to Oaxaca, but what are the chances?"

"I suppose I won't have to say much either, because the younger women are taught to keep quiet."

Rachel was barely listening to her again. "Why don't you finish packing. I'll forge our documents?"

Lauren felt dismissed. "Don't you think we should talk to Ben about the plan?"

"Yeah, I'll call him in."

When told the scheme, Ben's voice was incredulous. "But you told me not to lie."

"I know I did. But sometimes lying is the only thing that can keep you safe."

Ben practiced his lines, "Hablo Mixtec solamente. No hablo Inglés. No hablo Español."

Lauren squeezed his shoulder, and he didn't pull away. Lauren considered this a win.

After the documents were done, Rachel and Ben finished loading the van. Lauren changed into the prim gown, light pink with a starched white apron. It took quite a few bobby pins to get her short hair in a bun. When she was dressed, she couldn't believe the image in the mirror. "I guess Bryan finally got what he wanted." She laughed so hard she surprised herself.

Rachel came into the room and giggled. "I'm sure you feel ridiculous. But this *is* going to work." Lauren crossed her fingers.

In Our Bones

Slip Away

Rachel would have preferred to leave at nightfall to avoid the neighbor's prying eyes, but she didn't feel they had the luxury of time. She'd gleaned some information about what was going on with the checkpoints and found out that militias were on the move across the country. Rachel wanted to put as much distance between them and this particular militia group as fast as possible. They hurried into the van as Rachel took one last look at the home she'd been so proud to purchase. There will be time to mourn later, she told herself.

Lauren grabbed the Bible off Rachel's shelf and wedged it between the windshield and dash to keep it from sliding around. Lauren considered it both a prop and her guiding light. Rachel pulled out of her garage and started down the potholed street toward the nursing home where their mother had been living for the past five years. Skeletal remains of trees long perished lined the streets. They rolled past the restaurant where their parents had first met. One side of the building was scorched, and the windows were broken. Lauren grimaced. She was worried about seeing her mother. It had been a few months, and Ann hadn't recognized her the last time. It had so pierced Lauren's fragile spirit that she hadn't gone since. Lauren knew that Rachel judged her for that, too.

As Rachel pulled into the lot of the squat, one-story building, Lauren scanned for wayfarers. There were only two other cars there, one of which had a tree growing up through its trunk and weeds in every crevice. The door to the building was propped open, and the sisters exchanged a glance of distress.

Lauren said, "I don't want Ben to have to go in there. Just let me do it. Okay? You've done so much for her already." Lauren decided that she would fight her omnipresent guilt with action.

"Are you sure you can handle it? I mean, you've been through a lot."

"To be honest, I'm not sure. But I think I should try."

"Okay but come get me if you need anything."

As Lauren approached the door, a sickly rotten smell billowed out. She steeled herself for what she might find inside. There was no one at the front desk, but several residents were sitting in wheelchairs stripped down to dirty t-shirts and underwear. They didn't look up. Others were incoherently milling about the common room. The place was sweltering. Lauren covered her nose with her hand.

"Hello! Is there anyone here in charge here?" she called out. No one answered. Lauren continued down the hall toward her mom's room with a sense of foreboding. Glancing in doors as she walked, residents were lying in their beds listless. When she arrived at Ann's room, Lauren knew that something was wrong immediately. The sheets were gone from the bed and there was no sign of her mother. She wondered with a rising panic what that smell was? Lauren rushed toward a voice down the hall. She came across a short woman with coal-colored hair standing over a shell of a shockingly pale, old, white woman. The stubby woman was wearing a soiled nurse's uniform with the name Bi'ch on a pin. The nurse said in a thick Vietnamese accent,

"There you go, Mrs. Anthony. You'll be a lot more comfortable now." The room was disheveled with soiled laundry and food containers. Bi'ch looked up surprised to see Lauren.

"Hello there. Who're you here for?"

Lauren was near tears. "My mom. I mean Ann Hansberry. She wasn't in her room." She averted her eyes from the shrunken woman swimming in her baggy shirt.

Bi'ch's face fell and her voice grew sorrowful. She kept working. "I am so sorry, Miss...?"

"Lauren."

"I'm sorry, Miss Lauren. I have very bad news for you. Your mama, she passed three days ago. You've been on our list to call. But as you can tell, things have been crazy around here." She paused for a moment as she grabbed a food bowl from the counter and started feeding the ghostly woman. "I always did like your mama. She had that sparkle in her eye right up to the end. That last night she was doing so good, too. I stopped in for a sec to check on her. She asked me for some water, but all we got is this nasty stuff since the city worked on the pipes last week. They say it's just fine, and they ain't gonna do nothin' about it. These poor people. I did give your mom a few sips, but she didn't want more. The power has been touch-and-go, and there was no air conditioning the night she died. I think she just got too hot and dehydrated."

Lauren was listening but felt part of herself detach from the words. She was collapsing in on herself again. She struggled to remain present; she wanted to be able to handle this.

Lauren choked out, "Where is she now?"

"It's so sad to not be able to say goodbye, but we had to get her to the morgue as soon as we could. This heatwave's really been hard on folks. We lost five residents this past week, including your mama. We have to get 'em outta here as soon as we can. I don't mean to be insensitive, but Mr. Jensen died yesterday morning, and they ain't got him yet. You can smell what that's like. We didn't have a choice, Miss Lauren. I wish I could've done different for your family."

The news of her mother's death crashed together with the scent of it, and Lauren felt her stomach lurch. She scuttled down the hall back outside and dropped down to the hot pavement and dry heaved. Her legs were burning under her and forced her back to her feet. She rubbed her scorched shins as tears streamed down her cheeks. Ann had been a hard woman, but she hadn't deserved this. She shouted, "Mom... I let you down."

Rachel saw her and came hurrying. "What's wrong?"

"She's gone. She died three days ago. She's gone, Rachel."

"I should have gotten here sooner. Dammit! I didn't want her to die alone." She grabbed Lauren in a fierce embrace. Lauren let herself fold into her sister as they both wailed.

Bi'ch heard them and wandered out. "There you are! I was worried about you. How're you doing?"

Rachel straightened herself up. "Hi, I'm Ann's other daughter. I guess I'm shocked. It seems like everything's really fallen apart here."

Bi'ch harrumphed. "Yeah... it's a mess. I don't know how much longer I can last. My knees are giving me so much trouble."

Rachel said, "Are you here alone? How can you be expected to take care of everyone?"

"There's three of us working here still, but I'm alone today. I was supposed to be working with Valeria. But..." Her voice dropped, and she took on a conspiratorial tone. "Valeria and her sister both worked here. I didn't even know they were illegals! But I guess someone found out and burned down their house. They just up and left the city. The nursing home owner is so cheap, she won't hire anyone else. Since the Social Security got cut, she's not making any money. I think she just wants them all to die so she can be done. It's a shame, it is."

Lauren could not imagine the crushing pressure of what Bi'ch was describing. Part of her wished that there was something she could do to help, but more so she was glad that she could leave and never look back.

"I really appreciate everything you did for my mom," she said. "It helps knowing that she had someone like you around."

The sound of a resident moaning floated outside. Bi'ch said as she rushed off, "I've got to take care of this. Go ahead and take what you want from her room."

Rachel asked Lauren, "Do you think you can? Or would you rather I do it?"

Lauren swallowed hard. "I'm okay. I've got this."

Lauren went back to Ann's disheveled room, where she was more interested in soaking up the last of her mother's lingering energy than going through her stuff. The room was spartan, with few personal items aside from photographs assembled on the bedside table. Lauren stepped over to the rusted hospital bed and thought of her mom dying there. She gripped the bed rail and tried to steady herself. She saw the framed picture of her, Rachel and Ben and picked it up. Though only taken seven years before, it was as if it were a different era. Ben was small, only a few years old. Lauren recalled the day it was taken.

Up on the hill behind the farmhouse where Lauren grew up, Ann burst out exuberantly. "Would you look at that view!" She was radiant in the golden sunshine. "Isn't this a gorgeous day, Laur? Why don't we come up here more often?"

"Busy, I guess. It is pretty, though, isn't it? Look at that butterfly milkweed." Pure white butterflies were busily drinking nectar from the dazzling orange blossoms.

"Should we pick some?" Ann's mood was fine, and Lauren smiled as she'd asked rather than commanded.

They didn't know that Alzheimer's had already been picking away at her brain. Dale had only passed a few years before, and the heart of their family had gone with his death. But on this day, mother and daughter giggled like girls as the collected bouquets. Hiking back down the deer path to the house, Lauren allowed herself a hint of aspiration that things would get better between them.

Lauren adored the prairie her father restored. As a kid she'd spend hours there collecting bugs and petting the cows that grazed there. His pastures were Dale's pride. He'd say, "We don't need fancy technology to fix climate change, we just need more grasslands and trees. Instead we're always chasing the next shiny object that's supposed to fix it all. We can't buy our way out of this problem; we've got to plant our way out." Sitting in the blistering fever of the nursing home, Lauren finally understood why he'd cared so much.

In Lauren's memory of that day with her mom, Ben broke free from Rachel as soon as they came into view. He toddled over to Ann and buried his nose in the large bunch of flowers she'd collected. "Pitty Gama," he said with yellow pollen sticking to his face. They all laughed.

"They sure are pretty. Should we put these in water?" Ann grabbed Ben's hand and they headed inside. Lauren wanted to remember her mom just how she looked that day.

Lauren began removing the pictures out of their frames for easier transport. Lauren almost didn't take the photograph of herself but decided that Rachel might want it and be upset if she'd left it behind. As she removed the back of the frame, a neatly folded note fell out. In Ann's handwriting it read, "I will always love you." Lauren held the note to her and felt a surge of love for Ann unlike anything she'd felt when she was alive. Lauren finally understood that Ann did love her, and she must have known how brokenhearted Lauren was believing that she didn't. Lauren kissed the spot on the bed where her mother had crossed over and said, "I will always love you, too." She felt years of angst slip away.

As they drove through town to merge onto the highway, Lauren became numb. She was leaving behind everything she'd ever known and had no idea where their journey would take them. But an unexpected calm washed over her as she watched the Clinic's tall buildings recede in the distance.

Bryan might have her house, but he did not have her soul.

In Our Bones

Crystals in the Street

The night Bryan locked Lauren in the shed, he came back into the house to further humiliation from Steven, who had turned into a two-bit dictator overnight. He refused to let him get Lauren, even with the storm picking up. Bryan wanted to bring her food, but Steven said, "Hunger has a way of teaching lessons." Bryan worried about her in the way that a narcissist worries about the continuation of his supply. He loved the idea of her, not Lauren as an actual person with her own needs and wants. He loved the way she made him feel in control. Now with Steven, everything was spinning beyond him, and he didn't know how to make it stop.

In the morning, Bryan was given permission to bring her inside. He hurried through the backdoor only to see his green recliner burning on top of a pile of other items from the house. He forced himself to keep walking and stay quiet. Branches and refuse were scattered throughout the yard. As Bryan rounded the corner of the barn, he panicked when he saw that the shed had collapsed. He ran to start pulling off boards and debris, expecting to find Lauren's shattered body. After he cleared the pile, and she wasn't there, he started searching nearby. He was pissed. Though his predominant emotion was terror at how Steven would react to the news.

Bryan moped back to the house, passing the crushed path of daisies as he went. He thought of his grandmother and wondered what she'd think of him if she knew. They'd been her favorite flower. Without exception, she believed he was better than he ever was. She'd raised him after his mother died unexpectedly in a car crash when he was just twelve. His dad had taken off when he was a baby, so there was no one else. Tending a garden of rage throughout his life was an antidote to experiencing his pain; Bryan believed that opening his heart meant nothing more than suffering.

Bryan found Steven sitting at the head of the table in what used to be Lauren's dining room. A group of ten sycophants surrounded him and hung on his every word. When Bryan came in, Steven smirked. Bryan felt like such a coward for being afraid of him. He had expected to become part of the core leadership of the Defenders once they'd taken over the house. Instead, Steven was determined to break him down and prove that Bryan was no threat to his authority.

Steven barked, "What are you doing skulking around back there. What do you want?"

Bryan clicked his heels and put his arm straight out. "Sir, Commander, I have bad news. The shed gave way in the storm, and Lauren seems to have escaped. There's no sign of her."

Steven replied, "Fuck that whore. I don't care. We've got more important things to think about. Go get me a beer." Bryan followed his orders.

Steven's right-hand man was leading the conversation in the dining room. "We got word this morning about the next steps. They're calling it Project Blitz, and it sounds like a whole lot of fun!" The others around the table chortled. "Patriots in every state will converge on targets in the largest cities. There will be no question who's in charge after this. We're going to be working with other groups on how to proceed. Steven and I are meeting tomorrow with Minnesota's Patriot Coordinating Council. Today, we thought that we could do some planning on our end. So, ladies, let's do what those fucking eggheads call 'brainstorming'. What are the most important targets in the Twin Cities?"

The men frothed at the mouth as they considered the people they most wanted to hurt. They threw out the names of synagogues, mosques, cultural centers frequented by Hispanics, Somalis, Hmong and other minorities, Mormon Temples, liberal Catholic and other Christian churches, women's clinics, organizations for queer people, and the shopping districts and neighborhoods they considered fair game. Their glee was palpable.

Bryan was alone in the kitchen so no one could see him cringe. He'd joined up with these guys because he liked the power and control that it gave him. It was also important to him that scum knew their place and stayed out of the way of real Americans. But what they were talking about was something else entirely. He swallowed hard. *What about the kids?* The only tender spot left in Bryan's heart was for children. He needed to get some air. Bryan walked outside and briefly considered getting in his car and driving far away as fast as he could. He could find Lauren and tell her how wrong he was and how sorry he was. But he quickly discarded that fantasy. Steven had made it clear that the Defenders was a lifelong commitment. It was too late to object now. Whether he liked it or not, he was part of them.

Days passed, and he had gained no more esteem in Steven's eyes. The planning for Project Blitz continued, and the details turned his stomach. When the call finally came through that it was time for implementation, Bryan pushed down his feelings of nausea. They were at war, the guys said. It was kill or be killed. That's what Bryan told himself the day of the action as he put on a shirt the color of dark blood. He climbed into one of the waiting matching black trucks but didn't join in their war whoop. Bryan put in his headphones and stared blindly out the window. He decided that the only way to survive was to shut off the part of himself that cared about anything. He'd been doing that his whole life, anyway.

Some in their group were assigned to synagogues and mosques. Others rallied at the Hispanic Cultural Center. His team was assigned the Empowerment Place, a nonprofit that helped women and girls obtain an education. They pulled into the parking lot where five or six other matte-black vehicles of all types were already parked. Local police cordoned off the area. The men gathered around a tall skinny guy with a big pot belly that made him look as if he was pregnant. The man standing next to Bryan cracked a joke about it. "Are we sure this guy isn't really a harpy? Looks like he's carrying someone's bastard!" Bryan forced a nervous laugh.

The pot-bellied guy climbed onto a tailgate and started squawking. "We are here today to show these femoids that men are the righteous leaders of this country! Am I right?" The group started shouting "ER, ER, ER, ER!" in honor of the man Elliot Rodgers who was considered a saint among women-hating men everywhere because of his murderous rampage. His biggest fans were among a group that had gained considerable power in this new world order. They called themselves INCELS - involuntarily celibate. They blamed biology, but mostly they blamed women because no one wanted to have sex with them. This group decided that killings and rape were justifiable as a result.

The man went on. "We are not sniveling cowards, and we're taking our power back. We don't need any nasty roasties dragging us down and turning us into a bunch of weak cucks. We are strong, and we will take them down!" Chants of "ER" broke out again. The toxic energy was tapping into Bryan's fury. His face reddened as he joined in. Someone threw a bottle at the building, shattering it into a million glistening pieces. The group was whipping themselves up into a fervor.

The man in charge shouted, "It's time! Crush them! Burn these cunts down!"

Hate and testosterone swelled together as they stormed the building.

Bryan took his club and began smashing windows as the people inside howled. Within minutes every window was shattered, and the mob was throwing Molotov cocktails inside. Shards of glass glittered in the sunlight like crystals in the street. Women, men, and girls began running out as smoke and flames engulfed the structure. Sticks and fists greeted them as they fled for their lives. Bryan noticed someone slip away in the mayhem and almost make it around the corner. He chased after her with all the hostility-fueled adrenaline his body could muster. She had a head start and was getting away. Bryan reached down and picked up a chunk of broken concrete and chucked it at her. The rock struck her on the side of the head, and she fell with a thud. A Jackson Pollock-like splatter of red surrounded her on the sidewalk. Bryan bounded up to her limp body and funneled his bitterness toward his mother for dying, toward Lauren for leaving him, and toward Steven for making him feel small. Bryan thrust his foot again and again into the girl as she breathed her last breath. Only then did the rage drain away.

Bryan pushed her over with his tall leather boot. Blood streaked her platinum blonde hair, and her hazel eyes stared up at him. She looked a lot like Lauren from pictures he'd seen when she was a girl. A *girl. She's a child.* He shrieked, *Don't pussy out now!* Bryan jogged back to the rampage with as much zeal as the rest.

Back at Headquarters, they regrouped and held an exuberant bonfire party to celebrate their successes. Steven spoke to his soldiers with rare approval.

"Tonight, you became warriors for our cause. You proved your worth. You proved that you are real men who will protect those who are worthy. *Our* faith. *Our* heritage. *Our* women. *Our* children. And we will crush anyone who stands in our way!"

Arms went up as they chanted in unison, "Sieg heil, Sieg heil, Sieg heil."

The last of Lauren's beer and liquor were brought out and mind-numbing drugs circulated throughout. A handful of wives and girlfriends came, and the group cranked Aryan thrash metal. Bryan slammed down half a bottle of apple wine and smoked something that made him feel like he was hovering above the crowd. He took another hit whenever the girl's eyes popped into his mind. He had to stay numb.

A smaller group opted for a different kind of celebration. Instead of partying, they held a solemn prayer meeting inside the house. They'd taken special pride at the attacks on infidels at a Catholic church, a synagogue and a mosque. Unlike those outside, they'd washed and said their grace before a proper evening meal. They said *please* and *thank you* to their mothers, sisters, and wives as they set steaming plates before them. The women grinned and gushed with pride. The leader of the religious wing of the Defenders was a muscular man. He had small eyes with bushy eyebrows that made him look like a Muppet. He stood before his flock holding his well-worn New Testament.

"Brothers, your acts today showed your love of God. You are among the chosen ones who will usher in a new era of peace and prosperity across the land. Do not falter in your commitment. Do not forget your mission. Our work is ordained by the Lord Jesus Christ himself, brothers. Do not worry about the sinners outside who are having their lust-filled fun. Let them drink their wicked drinks and dance to their profane music. For we are ascendant. Very soon we shall take the righteous authority that God intended for us to have. When we are called to serve, we will bring the glory to the sons of Adam across the land. Let us read together the wisdom of Romans 13:

Let everyone be subject to the governing authorities, for there is no authority except that which God has established. The authorities that exist have been established by God. Consequently, whoever rebels against the authority is rebelling against what God has instituted, and those who do so will bring judgment on themselves. For rulers hold no terror for those who do right, but for those who do wrong. Do you want to be free from fear of the one in authority? Then do what is right and you will be commended. For the one in authority is God's servant for your good. But if you do wrong, be afraid, for rulers do not bear the sword for no reason. They are God's servants, agents of wrath to bring punishment on the wrongdoer, Therefore, it is necessary to submit to the authorities, not only because of possible punishment but also as a matter of conscience.

Amen.

In Our Bones

Flashing Lights

Lauren turned away each time a convoy of drab black vehicles sped by. She wished they hadn't changed drivers, but Ben was upset and needed Rachel to sit in the back with him. Lauren felt very alone as she drove. She hadn't thought of cigarettes much for weeks, but suddenly could think of little else. She was on overload and wanted the old familiarity of the burn. A gas station came into view up ahead, and Lauren couldn't take her eyes off it. She knew what Rachel's reaction would be if she asked to stop; she knew it was stupid to take a risk, but the call of tobacco was more than she could resist.

"Hey Rach, I was thinking of grabbing a pack of smokes. Is that okay?"

Rachel shot her head between the seats. "What are you talking about? No, you can't stop for cigarettes. What's wrong with you?"

Lauren didn't respond to her, but the thoughts kept frothing in her mind. It wasn't that Lauren didn't understand how toxic cigarettes were, but her addiction had been about the last thing she could deal with. She

147

was agitated that the craving had come back so suddenly and with such force. It had also struck Lauren that Rachel was particularly bitchy with her response. Lauren hated how Rachel always acted like she was so perfect and without flaw. *If only*.

Finally, Lauren decided to follow Rosa's advice and talk about hard things. "Why do you get so rude about smoking?"

Rachel sensed an argument coming, so she prompted Ben to pull out their decrepit iPad – all duct taped and barely maintaining a charge. When his headphones were safely in place, Rachel said, "Let's see... because it's disgusting. It's toxic, it's addictive, it stinks... I could go on."

"Yeah, but people do a lot of gross stuff that doesn't piss you off so much. I mean, it feels like there's something else. Like you devalue people who smoke, like they're worthless."

"I don't do that!"

"You kind of do. I mean, look at all the shit people are addicted to, that's destructive to themselves and others that doesn't make you pinch up your face like that."

Rachel considered the accusation for a good while before responding. "I don't know. Maybe you're right. But video game addictions don't put out poisonous smoke. If someone's addicted to pornography or whatever, it doesn't spill out into the world around them like tobacco."

Lauren was incredulous, thinking about Bryan's many dysfunctions and how they damaged her. "You've got to be kidding me, right? If someone is a gambling addict, let's say, and they spend all their money, you don't think that affects everyone around them?"

"You're right, I suppose. I hadn't thought of it that way."

"It just feels like almost everyone's hooked on something, but most people get a free pass because their issues are more hidden. No one glares at them when they walk by and makes snap judgments about who they are. I hate that. It's not like I truly love smoking or think it's an awesome thing to do. It's just hard to stop. And I wish you'd be more understanding." Lauren was pleased with herself. She had actually asked for something she needed. It felt good.

"I know it's hard. I actually feel that same way because of my weight. I should be more sensitive. Maybe it's a class thing that I'm not aware of. I'm sorry." Lauren thought, yeah, you got it. But she was thrilled to have an apology and forgave her. Rachel continued. "I hadn't really thought about all this before. I suppose I should focus on who I'm really angry with, and that's the tobacco companies. Their business certainly hasn't slowed down since the economy collapsed. In fact, it feels like everyone smokes again! Crazy. The companies make smoking seem all rebellious and sexy. Their ad men are so good. Did you know that they actually pulled their playbook from Big Oil? They're the ones who perfected the art of confusing the facts. They didn't need to convince anyone that smoking, or climate change weren't bad, only that the science was unclear how bad. It was all BS. That damned cigarette filter was the advertisers' invention, you know? Trying to convince people that there was a safe way to smoke. Just like they tried to convince everyone that we could keep pumping out carbon and methane with no consequences. I don't mean to judge you, but I still hate smoking."

"Fair enough. But thank you for hearing me." Lauren beamed; she'd stood her ground, and euphoria blunted her interest in having a cigarette.

They continued down the road for another hour, shooting past the Twin Cities. Lauren wondered if the alert about checkpoints was a rouse, as so many other statements by the government had been. Maximizing chaos was the Party's go-to strategy. Within minutes of that thought crossing Lauren's mind, flashing lights came into view. Lauren's blood ran cold. She shouted to Rachel, "Look!"

The highway had been eerily desolate and now a cacophony of action lay before them. They pulled in behind a row of three other vehicles, waiting for their turn through the checkpoint.

"Ben!" Rachel yelled, unintended anger in her voice. "Put down the iPad. Hide it under your seat." His eyes welled up. Rachel softened her tone. "I'm sorry. I didn't mean to yell. But this is serious. Remember what we talked about if we got pulled over? That's what's happening now. You don't speak English, right? Can you practice for me?" He did. "That's good. Now please pretend like you're sleeping and don't say anything unless you have to. No matter what. Okay?" Ben's eyes were wide and dazed as he took in their surroundings.

A car belonging to a Black family was pulled over to the side. Boys strapped with AK-47s who'd barely grown whiskers were ransacking it. Their belongings were strewn across the side of the highway. Lauren tried not to watch. She tried to stay focused on the task ahead. But when she stole a glance, her eyes locked momentarily with the woman. She was being shoved to the ground as a dog lunged at her. In an instant, Lauren felt as if the woman's horror were downloaded into her, just like she had with the teacher. She began shaking uncontrollably.

Rachel noticed and scooted in the front seat next to her. "What's wrong?"

"The eyes. It's the eyes."

"What are you talking about? You need to get it together!"

Lauren's brain shrieked, *Get out! Go help her. You have to help her.* "I can't handle this. I'm cracking up."

"You can handle this. You have to handle this, or we're lost. Get it together!"

Lauren white knuckled the steering wheel and took a deep breath. I am not weak.

Their van was next in line.

A boy with a clipboard and a large rifle determined the fate of each car. His name was Daniel and he had been born a soft-spoken gentle boy. He loved God, his country, and his family, in that order. Though he did what he was supposed to, he never liked it. Unlike some of the boys and men who reveled in their atrocities. Daniel had grown up in a tight-knit Christian Identity compound out in Spokane, Washington. It was run by ruthless con-artists who told their followers that they were ushering in the second-coming of the Lord. Their adherents and countless others like them saw the signs of the coming Apocalypse everywhere - locust swarms that brought famines, the pandemic, the fires of climate change, the American President relocating the embassy to Jerusalem. Their theology taught that God would descend to earth and send Jews and non-whites into enslavement in Heaven to serve their dead white overlords. White people would then have the Earth to themselves where peace would prevail. Daniel's parents had raised him and his nine siblings to adhere strictly to these tenets and sent him and his brothers out across the country as the militia movement grew.

Daniel often found that those he had to work with were not at all living the Godly life he had been taught to follow, though. He was certain the Lord was testing him. The only thing Daniel had in common with most of those he was assigned to was their "Boogaloo" war cry and desire to create a white ethnostate. Daniel's father cautioned patience whenever he'd complain, saying, "I know that they are apostates, son, and it's hard to live with all their fornication and sin. But for now, we need them. It's part of God's plan to bring forth the rise in the Adamic people. In the end, who will win? God will take his revenge in due time. The heretics will help us win this first battle, and then *we* will win the war." Daniel was also taught that proper white Christian women were to be revered. While women were expected to be submissive to men, they said it was not because women were inferior. Women were delicate, and men knew better how to shield them from the evils of the world. Daniel believed everything that he was taught, and that's precisely what Lauren had been counting on. She'd known enough men like him during her time with Bryan.

When they pulled up, Lauren's heart was beating so fast she thought it could explode.

Daniel politely asked, "Ma'am, where are you headed today? Do you know that there's a travel ban?" Lauren could tell by his tone that Daniel was naive and bought their act without question.

Lauren kept her eyes averted as she handed him the forged mission letter. "Yes. I do, sir. But we have to get this tonk child to his new home church immediately. They're in dire need of servants for our Lord." The words coming out of her mouth made Lauren want to vomit.

He studied the papers in the fading light of day and shined his flashlight at Rachel and Ben. Ben played his part perfectly. Lauren saw Daniel glimpse the Bible approvingly and stifled a smile. Another kid with a cocky expression staggered over smelling like a still. Lauren recognized him and fought the urge to step on the gas. He was one of the Defender's sons who she'd met a few times. The boy asked, "What's this here?" He grabbed the letter from Daniel's hands. Lauren had heard stories about this boy. She prayed he wouldn't recognize her and kept her head down.

Lauren guessed that the boozy kid was looking for a fuck, but she also guessed that Daniel wouldn't let that happen. Lauren could tell from his attitude with her that he took seriously his oath to protect the women of the Cross. Daniel yanked the paper from the other man's hands and looked him cold in the eye. "These sisters are cleared. Let them pass."

The kid ignored Daniel and put his face up to Lauren's. She could feel his breath on her cheek. "Hey, wait. Don't I know you?" the kid said to Lauren. Lauren didn't answer. "You're a pretty one, aren't you?" He reached out to touch her.

Daniel cocked his rifle and shoved the paper past the boy's face. "I said, these sisters are cleared."

The kid said, "You're such a priss, Dannie Boy. Don't ever want to have fun, do you?"

Daniel ignored him as he tipped his chin and waved them on.

Lauren gulped and said, "Thank you, sir," as she drove away.

When safely cleared, Rachel cheered, "We did it! You were awesome, sis."

Lauren grinned, "I did do it, didn't I?" She felt a warm glow, then remembered the woman on the road and it dissipated. She couldn't shake the feeling that there was something she should have done. "I'm not sure I can do it again, though. It's getting late. Should we find somewhere to pull off for the night?"

Rachel sighed. "I was hoping to get farther, but I suppose you might be right. I'll get out the Gazetteer and check for a good place – somewhere between towns where there's a lonely road that goes off by itself. We could even drive into a field, if we have to, the soil's so danged dry. I don't think it's rained since those big

155

storms came through." She stared at her tattered book of maps. "I might have found the perfect spot. It's not far from here. There's a road that branches off and goes about three miles before it stops at a river and what used to be a forest preserve. Who's going to be taking a road to nowhere?"

"That's perfect."

Rachel rubbed her chin. "Maybe a little too perfect. A lot of criminals are running logging and poaching operations. There could be something going on back there."

"How about we only go a half a mile or so in? Long enough that someone just turning around wouldn't see us, but hopefully not far enough in that anyone in the reserve would notice, either." Lauren hoped that she was right.

"Let's do it," Rachel agreed.

They pulled off the highway a few exits down. Years of periodic heavy rains had washed out the sides of the dirt road and created huge gullies. Driving was slow and dangerous.

Lauren spotted a collapsing barn and pointed, "There! We could pull in behind that." They drove the van as far behind the formerly glorious and now crumbling relic and switched off the lights. The sun hung low in the sky with ripples of purple and orange spreading across the horizon. Lauren felt like a mummy trapped in the long dress but was too frightened to step out of the van to change. Rachel pushed a few patches of screen she brought into small vents in the windows to keep the bugs out. Ben had fallen asleep a while before and stayed that way. Lauren and Rachel got as comfortable as they could.

Lauren tossed and turned on the reclined seat as she tried to settle her nerves. She'd fall asleep and jerk herself awake in panic. She kept seeing the woman in her nightmares. Shortly before dawn, a loud rapping on the window sent her up like a shot. Outside the van was a tall beefy man with a bandana on his head carrying an assault rifle. Lauren yelped. "What should we do?"

Rachel's eyes were huge and terrified as she grabbed her son. "We need to see what they want."

As Lauren gazed into Rachel's horror-struck eyes, she felt a wave of emotion flooding her again. She shut her eyes tight to quell them. She had to protect her family. "I'll go."

Ben cried, "No! They've got guns! What will they do to you?"

Lauren squeezed his hand. He cared. "We don't have a choice, honey. I'll be alright."

Climbing out of the van door, Lauren saw a woman and another man with rifles. The short man looked trigger happy, and Lauren tried to assess who these people were as her legs were wobbly.

The dew was thick in the dead brown grass and droplets of water glistened in the morning light. Swallows darted in and out of the barn devouring mosquitos. Lauren put her hands up and pleaded, "We're not here to cause any trouble. We were just camped overnight. I'll just get back in the van, and we'll leave you to your peace."

The short man laughed. "I don't think so, lady. That's not how this is going to work. You're in Resistance territory, and we don't take kindly to you folks delivering these kids into slavery."

Lauren had forgotten how she was dressed as she looked down at the long gown. The irony that what had saved them the night before could now get her killed didn't escape her. She winced. "There's been a mistake. I know you may not believe this, but the boy is actually my nephew, Ben. We put on these clothes to create a cover story to get past the checkpoints."

The woman was wearing fatigues and had a large pistol holstered to her side. She stepped forward and put her hand up. "I'll handle this."

The short man asked, "You sure, Jada? I say we take the kid and send these ladies to their Maker." Lauren froze.

Jada scolded, "Quit trying to scare her." She turned to Lauren, "How do I know what you just told me isn't your cover story?"

"He's the reason we left Rochester. It wasn't safe for him there since the militias were legalized. That's my sister, and we're trying to get him to Kanata. He'll tell you that what I'm saying is true."

Jada nodded, "Get him out."

Rachel and Ben stepped out of the van, trembling, and clinging to each other. Ben belted out his line, just like Rachel taught him. "No hablo Ingles."

Rachel said, "Sweetie, it's okay to say the truth this time. Please tell them that I'm your mom." Ben shook his head and buried his face in her belly. Rachel petted his head and looked at Lauren with panic.

Lauren saw the short man moving toward them and jumped in front. "It's the truth!" The man put his finger on the trigger. "Please, don't shoot! Can't you see he's scared? Ben, Ben. Look at me." She dropped to her knees in front of Ben. "You are so brave, and right now you are the only one who can save us." He started whimpering. "Please, baby. I know you're scared."

Hardly above a whisper he said, "This is my mom, Rachel, and my Aunt Lauren. Please don't hurt us."

The man in the bandana lowered his gun and bent down. "Son, are they making you lie? Because if these people are hurting you, we'll take you right now somewhere safe. You'll never see them again."

Ben howled, "Please, don't take them away!" as Lauren and Rachel began crying, their faces tortured.

They went on this way for a beat before Jada took charge. "Okay. I've seen enough. I believe them. Erik, Jerry, take them to the camp."

Lauren's mind swirled. "What? We can't go to the camp, whatever that is! We need to get back on the road. I don't understand. If you believe us, why won't you let us leave?"

Jada responded, "Because it's not safe for me to let you leave. I'm surprised you even made it this far. Yesterday the militias started their campaign of terror. They've got roadblocks and patrols everywhere, but especially across the border region. They don't want anyone escaping. What do you think they're going to do if this little act doesn't fool them? No offense, ladies, but I don't care much about you. I do care about that little boy, though, and he's under my protection now. Don't worry, we won't keep you here forever. We just need to let everything simmer down for a while." Then Jada spoke directly to Ben, "Sugar, you're safe with us. We're going to take care of you and your family." She put her hand on his shoulder. "There are lots of kids at the camp, and we've even got a nice little school."

At the word "school" Ben's eyes brightened.

Action, Not Guilt

As they crested the small hill shielding the camp from view, Lauren's face twisted. "It looks like a refugee camp."

"That's because it is," Rachel retorted.

The compound was situated in a narrow valley with a trickle of a river cutting through. Tents, shanties and vehicles were packed in tightly in the field, extending at least a mile. A menagerie of fencing blocked it off on three sides with the river making up the other border.

Shell-shocked, the three of them got out of the van and took in their surroundings. People of all sorts milled around. Some were working on their shacks, others were carrying water or talking together. Several people waved, but no one paid them much attention. Jada dropped off Erik and he approached them. His tone was kindly. "I'm sorry about all that back there. We just can't be too careful. Jerry's kind of a hothead. I hope you know we wouldn't have shot you."

Lauren took him in for the first time. He was gorgeous and, despite having just pointed a gun at her, she believed she'd found her next man. The month since Lauren had escaped Bryan was among the longest stretches she'd gone without a relationship. She batted her eyes, "It was pretty scary, but we're okay now."

Rachel was less forgiving. "That's a really horrible way to greet people. My kid is traumatized."

"I really am sorry, ma'am."

"Don't. Just don't. I'm not your mother."

Erik fumbled his words. "I didn't mean…"

Lauren thought that Rachel sounded exactly like their mother. She interjected, "Don't let her bother you. She gets grumpy."

Rachel snapped back, "I'm not grumpy. Don't you remember what just happened?"

While Rachel was talking Lauren noticed a trio of little girls popping in and out from the side of the van, giggling. The sight made Lauren's palms sweaty since all were wearing Khimar-style hijab, and Lauren had been taught to fear anyone who looked like that. She was sizing up how to react when an adult woman wearing a floral headscarf and long red skirt approached.

Erik called out in his Minnesota timbre, "Hiya, Marium." He said to Lauren and Rachel, "This is our esteemed doctor."

Lauren moved closer to Rachel with angst, but hoped she looked calm on the outside. All introduced themselves and Erik said, "Which one of you wants to go to the supply tent with me?"

Lauren both wanted to be with Erik and get away from Marium. She spoke quickly, "Me! But can I get changed first? I can't stand everyone thinking they know who I am based on this dress."

Marium sighed, "I know what you mean." Lauren colored as she realized the irony.

Suddenly a loud, "Tag" rang out. The oldest of the three girls tapped Ben on the shoulder running off laughing.

Ben's eyes were full of excitement. "Can I, Mom?"

Rachel answered nervously, "I suppose. Just stay where I can see you!"

Marium said, "Those are my girls. I guess that's obvious." She laughed.

Lauren looked at Marium and then at her daughters playing. They certainly didn't seem like terrorists. Lauren changed into her normal clothes and went with Erik to the massive canvas tent where they kept supplies. As they walked, Lauren mulled over his name. Why does he have to be named Erik? Lauren couldn't stand that name and avoided all Erics like the plague. The name made her skin crawl, thinking about what had happened all those years before. It's time to let that go, she told herself.

When they got to the supply area, Lauren marveled at the variety. "Where do you get all this?"

"We have crews going out once a week or so to pick through the abandoned buildings in the area."

"That actually sounds kind of exciting."

"It can be. Can be dangerous, too."

Lauren twisted up her mouth as she considered how to ask the question that had been on her mind since they arrived. "Speaking of danger... I noticed quite a few Muslims here. Don't you ever worry about that?"

Erik looked shocked. "We're all here for the same reason – to be safe. You need to check your bias at the camp's edge, because we're trying to make this a secure space for everyone. I'm not saying that the people here are all perfect. Uff da, we've got some jerks. But it isn't the Muslim people more than anyone else. If anything, it's probably the white men like me who never figured out how to share power with anyone but other white men."

Lauren was feeling so many things at the same time. She was ashamed to be criticized. But his voice hadn't been cruel. Even more so, she admired how he was standing up for people, not cowering in fear or lashing out like Bryan and the Defenders. Lauren was even more drawn to him than before and began shamelessly flirting. Erik was not reacting to her, though, and it confused Lauren. Few men failed to respond to her flirtation.

Erik asked, "How about your family join me tonight for dinner? The mess hall starts serving around five. Bring Marium, too. Since you'll be neighbors now, it'll be good for you to get to know her."

Lauren brightened. "Sure. How about five-thirty?"

"Perfect. Here's a cart to get your stuff back. I'll see you tonight."

Lauren pulled the heavy wooden cart across the compound, stopping frequently as she still tired easily, but she eventually got it back to the van. She and Rachel set up the tent and the rest of a makeshift camp while Ben scooted around with the other children. Lauren thought of what Erik had said about checking her prejudice, and she realized how much of it must lurk in her heart. She was the type of person who would have been offended had anyone said she was racist, because she would never be openly rude to someone's face. Hers was the kind that loitered in the interstices of her mind and heart, feeding on her fears and worries with little conscious awareness. Lauren heaved, thinking of the years of Bryan's hate-fueled indoctrination that she needed to unpack. Living up to her new mantra of action, not guilt, she jogged over to play with Ben and Marium's girls.

Marium was at the medical clinic next to their site when Lauren went over to invite her to the evening meal. Marium agreed and at the right time the party of seven set off to meet Erik. He was sitting near the door waiting for them. "Go ahead and get your food. I'll save the table." A long counter was set-up along the back wall filled with large pans of delicious-smelling foods. The Hansberrys hadn't eaten a real meal since the day before, and Lauren was ravenous. She took a plate from the stack, and Marium said, "We wash these ourselves after. I'll show you."

Lauren questioned, "They grow food here?"

"Yeah. They do. But I don't know much about it. I just stick to my doctoring."

Since Erik mentioned that everyone who was able was expected to join a work crew, Lauren decided that the garden would be her destination. Though, the idea of working for the team that collected stuff from empty buildings kept dancing in her mind. Lauren wasn't sure that she needed any more excitement after what she'd been through but had to admit that the adrenaline rushes had a certain intoxication.

When they joined Erik at the table, the adults sat together, and the kids sat nearby. It was like the kids had known each other their whole lives, Lauren thought. She wished it were as easy for adults. The mess hall was a network of cobbled together plywood filled with unmatched dining sets. It looked to Lauren like a used furniture store. She sat down next to Erik in an attempt to woo him some more. "So, what's your story?"

"Oh, that's a long one."

"We've got time." Lauren flipped her hair.

"Okay then. I grew up on the Iron Range and a lot of my friends were Party supporters. The militia in our area kept growing, and my buddies tried to recruit me. But I could see the President for who he was from the beginning. So, I steered clear. But when they started attacking people in my community, I couldn't sit back. I ingratiated myself to them, acting like I was their ally. I'd do crazy stuff to slow 'em down, like put laxatives in their food, disable their weapons, or putting detergent in their gas tanks. One night, some guy caught me red handed, and I took off then and there. I'd been hearing that this camp was forming, so I made my way here. Enough about me. What about you?"

Lauren wasn't sure how to react to what he'd said, but she was fairly certain that he wouldn't think too highly of her if he ever found out about Bryan. As Lauren spluttered with how to answer, Rachel jumped in. "We grew up on a farm in the southeast of the state. I suppose you can see we're a few years apart in age, but it's just the two of us now. I've been worried about my son for a long time, but once the militias were legalized, it didn't seem like we had much choice but to leave."

Marium groaned. "No, it's not safe for him. Nor for anyone who looks like him or me. My family and about fifty others banded together to create a little colony way out in the country by ourselves. We figured if we left everyone alone, they'd leave us alone. Wrong. We got raided and my husband was killed. My daughters and I hiked for days to find shelter. We got lucky when the Resistance gleaners found us and brought us here." Lauren felt sheepish considering how she'd reacted to Marium just a few hours before.

Rachel asked, "How long have you been here?"

"About six months. Erik here's been helping me get my medical clinic set up. I think he about peed his pants when he found out I was a doctor. There weren't any here before me."

Erik laughed, "There was absolutely no peeing involved. But yes, I was pretty stoked. You're about the best thing that's happened to this place."

Erik had a mature, in-charge energy that wasn't pushy. After Bryan's insecure posturing, Lauren found his confidence reassuring. Erik came across as someone who knew who he was and didn't need to prove anything to anyone. That's the way I want to be, she thought.

After their meal, the doctor took them down to the river to wash up. Lauren's nose crinkled at the foul oily water. Global, regional, and local conflicts over scarce water resources raged. The President ordered militia groups to secure access as a priority for their new headquarters buildings across the country. Rachel washed Ben as much as he'd allow, and the family walked back to settle in for the night. After Ben fell asleep, the sisters had their first chance to speak alone since coming.

Lauren asked, "Have you been thinking about Mom?"

"All day."

"I have too, but I can't seem to feel the way I should."

"You two had a hard relationship, and she was sick for a long time. I know I've been mourning since she was diagnosed. If we're being honest, all we've been through these past two days would have been too much for her. I'm sad she's gone, but I think more of me is relieved that she's with God now."

"Yeah, I guess all that's true."

"Grief unfolds over time, Lauren. Give yourself some space to work through it once things settle down."

Lauren said, "It feels like things will be okay now. I like it here."

"Me too, but I still think we should move along as soon as possible."

Lauren rolled over, sleepy. "We'll see."

Days rolled into weeks, which rolled into months and the Hansberrys fell into a routine. Rachel started helping at the clinic, and she and Marium were becoming fast friends. Lauren took up work in the gardens, as she'd hoped, and Ben attended school, as he'd hoped. Erik was around here and there, and Lauren would pull out all her allure. Lauren was frustrated that things weren't progressing and had to keep herself from finding another target. Rachel cautioned patience, saying Lauren needed more time to heal from Bryan. Reluctantly Lauren agreed to cool her heels and sought a different type of exhilaration than new love. She offered to go out on one of the trips with the procurement team. She was nervous as hell but wanted to contribute to the camp more than just weeding.

The next morning, Lauren awoke before sun-up to join the crew. The camp had converted a van to run on vegetable oil or animal fat they made into biodiesel. They'd been able to acquire enough from abandoned restaurants to keep their vehicles running without the need for gas. The dusty van drove for nearly an hour then pulled into a lot with a chipped sign that read, Boulder Ridge Apartments, though there were no boulders nor ridges to be seen. Four identical tan buildings in various states of disrepair stood before them.

Pedro, the crew leader, was energetic and his voice encouraging. Lauren liked him immediately. "Listen up. I'd like to finish buildings two and three today, if we can. Lauren, since you're new, why don't you stick with me?"

Four others grabbed supplies and went their own ways. Lauren held her breath as she and Pedro entered the doorway to the main hall. Dim light filtered in revealing plaster littering the floor and a fuzzy layer of black mold on the walls. The musty smell was nauseating. Pedro handed her a mask, "Here, put this on. We don't want to be breathing this stuff in."

"How do we know what we're looking for?"

"We keep an inventory of what we've got and what we still need. But if something seems really good, we just take it."

"It seems so strange to me to be picking through the remains of people's lives."

"You'll get used to it. You just have to keep telling yourself that the rules of survival have changed. It's not stealing. We're just taking things that would end up rotting here. We're giving it another life is all."

Lauren agreed, but couldn't help feeling creeped out by the entire enterprise. The first few apartments went quickly, with little to take. When they were going through the second apartment, Pedro let out a whoop. He was pouring over a stash of small dark brown bottles.

"Marium's going to be thrilled. These essential oils are gold. We use them for all sorts of things, but some are great antibacterials. Plant oils are most of what people used to treat infections before antibiotics were ever invented. People really screwed that up, though. Pumping farm animals so full of antibiotics is a lot of what created these goddamned super bugs. Sorry, I don't mean to drone on. I was a microbiologist in Honduras before my nephew and I came here."

Lauren was surprised, as she tended to think of immigrants as uneducated. "Why did you come if you had such a good job?"

Pedro scoffed, telling only part of the story. "The drug cartels killed my sister and tried to recruit my nephew. I couldn't let that happen, so we walked all the way to the border hoping for asylum. It was awful. There were so many kidnappings by other cartels, it was like we couldn't get away from them. Then the U.S. government quit accepting asylum applications, and we were just stuck in limbo at the border. And trust me, it was waaay worse than here. There were no bathrooms, water, nothing. Finally, my uncle paid to get us smuggled through a tunnel under the wall."

"Wow. That's horrible. I didn't realize how bad things were." Lauren felt uncomfortable, as if Pedro could know all the things she'd said and thought about immigrants. She doubled her efforts to be helpful. *Action, not guilt.*

At the last apartment on the top floor, Lauren opened the door to a bedroom and bellowed. "Pedro. Come here!"

Pedro examined the room. "I forgot to warn you about the bodies. Ah man. Poor guy. I've seen this a lot. Mostly old, sick and disabled folks ended up just getting left behind when no one could take care of them anymore. I find them in wheelchairs sometimes, too. It was like Darwinism by default. So sad. Let me do this. I know it's a lot for your first day." Lauren was about to argue that she could handle it, despite knowing she couldn't when the sound of an engine came through the window. A small truck with gaping rust holes stopped next to the van.

Pedro whispered, "I think those are the ones who broke in a couple of months ago and ripped off our stuff. I think they're on drugs. Son of a gun, I'd better go scare them off. They're getting nothing today."

Outside an emaciated man and women were tugging at the van's doors. Pustules covered their faces and arms.

Pedro aimed his rifle, "That's enough now. You two get outta here."

The man got a crazed look in his eyes and started yelling back, "Fuck you, prick. We've got just as much a right to this stuff as you."

Pedro shouted back, "You do the work bringing things out, you get to keep it. Those are the rules. Now go on."

The man rushed at Pedro, pulling a knife from his back pocket. A single shot took him down. The skinny woman squealed as she ran back to their truck and tore off, leaving her bloody dead companion in the lot. Lauren was confused because Pedro hadn't fired until she looked across and saw a woman about her age with a shotgun. Lauren had never seen someone be killed before and was horrified. She began piteously sobbing. Pedro didn't react to the man's death, instead he was looking down the road at a dark, tall, inverted funnel cloud. "Look there. It's a dust devil headed our way. Let's get the van loaded and get out of here. Go, go, go!"

The driver hit the gas as the mini tornado ripped through the parking lot, picking up the man's body and slamming it into the building. Lauren groaned. She didn't want to be cold, but she didn't want this crying all the time either.

The woman who'd done the shooting glared at her. "What's your problem?"

"Why did you kill that man? He probably would have taken off with a warning shot or blowing out his leg. He didn't have to die."

The woman was putting her hair up in a ponytail and flatly stated, "Listen, girlie. I don't ever like taking out anyone. But I'm not going to moralize over that junkie's death. If he'd have gotten Pedro even once, he could have killed him. If not from the cut itself, from the infection. No matter how many of those bottles of oil we bring back, it's not enough to treat a deep wound. Whatever drug they're on makes them lose their minds, and they get really strong. I wasn't gonna risk it. Pedro is more important than he is. Sorry, not sorry. You'll get used to it. Or not. I'm surprised Erik recommended you join us. You seem kinda fragile to me."

Lauren bristled. *I'm not fragile.*

Pedro interjected, "There's no two ways about it, this work is hard. When people are in impossible situations, they have to make impossible choices. Maybe you can't handle it. But you shouldn't feel bad that you're crying because someone died. I've just dealt with so much; I can't take it in anymore. But then that makes me feel awful, too. The trick is to somehow hold both sorrow and pragmatism in your heart and mind at the same time. The Yin and the Yang, sort of."

While her body jerked back and forth along the road, Lauren contemplated Pedro's words and knew he was right. She wondered if she'd ever be able to figure out a way to balance her emotions. She also wondered if she should stick to gardening.

Extinction

The shot rang out clear and thunderous as it tore through its intended target.

"Hell yes!" Lauren pumped her fist in the air. She focused the rifle again, and another bullet hit its mark. Erik will be so proud of me, she thought. Fuck that. I'm proud of me.

Pedro clapped her on the back. "Great work. Looks like I'm a good teacher."

Lauren tousled his hair, "Don't let your head swell up, you're just helping me work through the kinks. I've probably been shooting since before you were born, kid." Lauren's father was the type of man who believed in living his politics, with gender equality being a central factor. His daughters learned to shoot, hunt, fish and drive a tractor just the same as if he'd had sons.

"Don't call me kid," Pedro laughed. He pulled something from his pocket and handed it to Lauren.

"What's this?"

"A present. "

Lauren unwound a foot-long plastic wire wrapped around two handles. "Thanks. But what is it?"

"A garrote."

"And that is?"

"An ancient weapon used to kill with stealth. You wrap it around someone's neck, give it a good pull, and they're done."

Lauren frowned, "Yikes. That's horrifying. Thanks, but let's hope this is something I never need." She stuffed it in her back pocket, again wondering how a scientist knew so much about fighting and weaponry. "Should we get a bite? I'm dying."

"Sure…"

Lauren checked her phone. "Never mind. Can't. I forgot I promised Erik I'd help him with the security perimeter. Should we meet up the same time tomorrow?"

After that first day out with the scavengers, Pedro offered to help toughen Lauren up and they trained together regularly.

Lauren ambled back to her shack and hung the rifle up on its hook. She grabbed a snack and climbed on the four-wheeler to find Erik.

The Hansberrys' months at the camp had rolled into years. Erik continued to be skeptical of Lauren's romantic advances for a good spell. But his esteem for her grew as he saw her transforming from the person she was to the person she was becoming. Erik liked this woman appreciably better than the one he'd first met. Ironically, when Erik was ready to love Lauren, she wasn't able to accept him. At first, being alone was excruciating for her. Little by little, she realized that she needed that space to learn who she actually was. She'd never been able to sit with herself long enough to have the difficult conversations within her heart. She maintained her single status for nearly a year until she'd reconciled enough of the indecisions and contradictions within herself that she felt centered enough to truly love someone. To Lauren, love was no longer simply clinging to another, but it was giving all she had while not losing herself in the process. Once she understood, she was ready to accept Erik and to tell him about Bryan and the Defenders.

Erik handled Lauren's need for time well. He didn't push or pout as so many of the men Lauren had known before. She and Rachel both considered this a sign of his character. Lauren came to rely on Rachel's counsel in all matters, but in particular with relationships. The two of them still had their annoyances with each other but had a firm basis for growth.

After Lauren decided that she was ready to tell Erik her story, she needed to find a good time to do so. In the Fall of that year, Erik and Lauren gathered with others around a campfire to take the edge off the chill in the night air. The two of them were lingering behind the others, and their spark was crackling along with the fire. Lauren hated to spoil the mood but couldn't hold out any longer. She launched into her account, and to her relief, Erik was understanding and gentle. He held her tight as she divulged her second biggest secret, and she felt like a million pounds had lifted from her shoulders.

After Lauren was finished, Erik shocked her with a secret of his own. He took in a long breath before he began.

"I realize more of what you're saying about Bryan than you know. He sounds like a narcissist, and if there's one thing I know, it's narcs. I was married before. I know I don't talk about her because of how awful it was, but we were together for fifteen years. It started out great, just like with you and Bryan. After we got married is when everything changed. She started putting me down, acting like I was an idiot, all that stuff. At first, I ignored her, but then she started throwing things at me and screaming all the time. She had a lot of medical problems, so I tried to be understanding. But most of the time I was just tired and confused. She was one of the President's biggest fans, I'm telling you. I think because they acted just like each other – all the lying, gaslighting, blaming everyone else for everything, thin skin, the whole nine yards. I should have divorced her, instead I tried to stay away from home as much as I could. She didn't want a husband; she wanted a punching bag. Nothing I ever did or said was good enough. We both got COVID, but I was hardly sick. She went into the ICU and needed a ventilator, but our rural hospital ran out. They couldn't get her to the Cities in time. I felt terrible, like I'd willed her to die." He cleared his throat to keep his tears at bay. "It's funny that part of me feels bad telling you now. Like I'm betraying her. Or maybe I'm just embarrassed still."

Lauren took his head in her hands, looked deep in his soft blue eyes and gave him a long and tender kiss. He let himself cry, and afterward the two of them were inseparable.

Lauren rolled up on the quad runner and found Erik reinforcing a section of the camp's fence. There had been several minor incursions from gangs and militias, but the federal government had left them alone. For several weeks now, the camp was on high alert as government drones began flying overhead. Everyone was on edge.

Erik was dripping with sweat, even though there were a few inches of snow on the ground. Lauren said, "What needs doing here?"

"We're adding this rebar to the slats, hopefully making it a little stronger. Between you and me, this isn't going to do anything if they want in."

"At least it's making people feel better."

"Yep, that's why I'm doing it. Did you get the bug-out bags ready?" They were putting together supplies for a quick departure if the camp was raided.

"I did. One for us, one for Rachel and Ben and another for Marium."

The tent that Lauren and Rachel started with had given way to two tiny one-room shacks built next to Marium's clinic. One for Rachel and Ben, and another for Erik and Lauren. Marium and her girls and Erik and the Hansberrys formed a family of sorts. By the time it was safe to continue the journey to Kanata, Ben and Lauren had convinced Rachel to stay. Nacia felt further away with each passing day. Ben went to school with Marium's daughters and her oldest, Khadija, was his best friend. Rachel began working as Marium's nurse, receptionist, and gopher. Lauren not only continued with the procurement team after that crazy first day, in time she became co-leader along with Pedro. Pushing past fear was her new hobby, and she vowed never to forget how it had once controlled her. She'd mostly worked through the relentless drumbeat of guilt she experienced, but still had a tendency of swinging wildly from sadness to shut down. She tried to be gentle with herself; as Pedro had said, *it takes time.* She'd mostly dismantled the high wall in her mind that separated thought from feelings. Instead she'd learned to create flimsier structures that held the worst back long enough to get a grip. Lauren still cried frequently, but for moments only.

Lauren was pleased that she was able to start channeling her empathy into a force for good, though, and no longer descending into blubbering as much. She could observe and anticipate what others needed, often bringing back items from procurement trips that someone hadn't known they even wanted. She also found skills she didn't know she had in improving the camp's design and infrastructure. From growing up on a farm, Lauren seemed to know a little of everything. The accomplishment of which she was most proud, though, was creating a specialized unit that gleaned old gardens for seeds and plants that could be brought back to the camp's farm. Lauren wasn't officially a leader at the camp, but she'd become indispensable.

That evening after supper, snow fell in fat wet clumps outside. Lauren was considering calling it a night, and Erik was snoozing nearby in their cozy one-room shanty. She yawned and rubbed her eyes before rising to put another log in their makeshift wood stove. The sounds of drones and approaching vehicles were muffled from the snow, and Lauren was unaware of their presence until a vast explosion echoed through the compound. The camp's artillery and rocket launchers began firing back as Erik sprung up.

They hurried to put on their coats and boots, as Erik gave her a brief embrace. "Let's follow our plan. I'll head over to Rachel's. I love you. I'll see you soon."

Lauren hoped that this was true as the thought of losing him was more than she thought she could endure.

"I love you, too," she whispered.

Lauren scurried outside as flames were consuming the camp, and drones were shooting from overhead. Soldiers with spotlights on their helmets were everywhere. Lauren felt someone grab her, and before she could think she stuck her knife deep in his belly. She pushed him, and he let her go, gripping his abdomen. Lauren rushed on and burst through the open door of the medical clinic. Khadija's shrieking inside was excruciating, and Lauren ran as fast as she could down the hall to the family's quarters. Inside their apartment, Marium's body was crumpled on the floor with a bullet wound in her head. *Oh, Marium!*

A fat man had Khadija pinned down and was fumbling with his zipper as she was beating him in the face. Lauren's mind went black. She couldn't shoot and her knife would be difficult. She pulled the garotte Pedro made her from her pocket as she quietly made her way to the scene. Lauren slipped the weapon around the man's throat and yanked as hard as she could. He'd never seen her coming. He began flopping and grabbing his neck as Khadija kicked him away and crawled out from beneath him. Lauren's back was to the door, and she didn't see two more men barge in. Khadija did see them, though, and grabbed the dead man's automatic rifle, sending a spray of bullets across the room. She shrieked and threw the gun down.

Lauren shouted, "Where are your sisters?"

"I don't know! They took them. My mom was trying to protect them when they shot her."

"There's no way for us to find them. I'm sorry. We have to go right now." Lauren picked up the gun and grabbed Khadija firmly by the arm.

"We can't leave without them. No!" Khadija fought to get away.

Lauren used her harshest tone to snap her to reality. "We can't save them! We'll be lucky if we save ourselves. Grab your bag."

Khadija's eyes were pools of grief as they stepped over Marium's body. She wailed, "Forgive me."

As Lauren dragged Khadija out the door, she thought, goodbye dear friend. Khadija buried her face in Lauren's back on their way down the hall. Before they went out, Lauren said, "You've got this. Okay? Just stick with me."

Khadija nodded and grasped Lauren's hand tightly, dodging their way through the mayhem to the corpse of trees not far from their cabins. Erik, Rachel, and Ben were waiting. Khadija ran to Rachel who'd become almost a second mother to her. Lauren said, "We need to move."

Rachel screeched, "Where's Marium and the other girls?"

Lauren's voice cracked, "Dead, gone. We need to go, right now."

Explosions and blood curdling screams could be heard as they sprinted through the narrow row of woods into the adjacent forest. After they'd reached the hill overlooking the camp, they could see fire consuming the remaining structures as the bedlam continued. Lauren wondered about Pedro and thought of Marium and her girls. A fissure of pain began opening up in her that she stitched shut immediately. As Rachel would say, there would be time to grieve later.

The bug-out bags were well-packed with supplies Rachel had brought when they'd first fled Rochester, as well as other items Lauren collected from her time with the crew. They pushed on through the night, and toward daybreak Erik spotted a zigzag of downed trees with a perfect hollow for them to rest. They laid out their foil sleeping bags and huddled together in terror. Khadija had never spent a night away from her family, and her grief was inconsolable.

Lauren and Erik slept in shifts to stand guard. She took the first, eyes wide and gripping her rifle fiercely. Each crack of a stick or rustle of leaves put her on alert. Her stomach churned as she recalled the warm blood on her hands. Inside she was emotionally void. She couldn't stop herself from rebuilding the wall in her mind because it was all too much, but this time she remembered to add a door.

The group stayed away from roads and navigated the semi-frozen marshlands and lakes to make their way north. Nacia was the destination if they could get there. They'd been traveling for days, and their feet were perpetually wet and blistered. Their rations were enough to keep them alive, but not more. Hunger burned in their bellies. Lauren's canteen was nearly empty, and she was hoping to find somewhere to fill it when a small stream appeared ahead.

"Let's stop for a minute, okay?"

Rachel was the first to get there and plopped down. She put her bottle in the water and began drinking deeply to ward off the bite in her stomach. Lauren was filling hers when she spotted a dead deer with its face touching the water a few feet upstream. Lauren said, "Stop drinking. There's a dead animal there. Let's move on."

Rachel spit out the water in her mouth, and everyone dumped their containers. They began hiking up the creek to get around the dead deer when Ben spotted another. Then Khadija. As they looked around, everyone's eyes were wide. An entire herd of deer lay rotting in the scrub around them.

Lauren hissed, "Holy…"

Rachel's face fell. "Anthrax, I'll bet. Dammit. We need to get away from here. Kids don't touch anything. Don't put your hands near your face!"

Lauren yelped, "Anthrax! I doubt it. That's rare."

Rachel scratched her head. "Used to be. It's pretty common now that the tundra's melting and releasing spores from all these long-frozen carcasses."

Erik said, "That's what I was thinking, too. Let's backtrack the way we came."

Khadija confided, "Everything about the woods scares me. It reminds me of when we were lost after the raid on my family all those years ago. This is déjà vu."

Rachel gave her a squeeze. "I'm so sorry, honey. Come here and walk by me."

Ben declared, "I'm not scared of the woods. I'm scared of people. I hope we see some bears."

Lauren looked at Rachel and back at Ben. A hard lump grew in her throat as Rachel fumbled for words.

"I should have told you sooner, I know that now. We won't see any bears."

"Why not?"

Rachel answered, "Because there aren't any in the wild anymore. They're extinct. With winters so warm, it messed up their hibernation. They needed food year-round, but there wasn't enough because the whole ecosystem was changing. Many starved. Diseases took their toll, as you can see with those deer, and people hunted the rest. I didn't have the heart to tell you."

Ben's voice dropped and he hung his head. "That makes me feel really icky. You're right, you should have told me." He straggled behind. Lauren wanted to go to him but figured he could use some time to himself.

Mass extinctions and the collapse of ecosystems had torn away at Rachel's spirit more than almost any other tragedy of their mutated world. Rachel wanted the Earth as it once existed to remain alive in Ben's mind like a fairy tale for as long as she could get by with it. The conversation about the planet's destruction had brought a pall over the group, as if it had tapped out the last of their energy. They hiked in silence for a long while. Lauren could see Rachel's despondency and wanted to comfort her but had little left to give.

Lauren worried more about Ben, though, as she watched him trudge along the burned stubble. Gangly young trees hoping to survive the next wave of forest fires dotted the topography. The landscape had been shaped and reshaped over and again by humans and forces beyond humanity for millennia. Those arguing that global warming was of no concern because changes were perpetual never understood that was beside the point. Were the changes good or bad, and were they avoidable? Those were the questions that needed to be asked and weren't.

Eventually they plodded out of the scorched area and entered an expanse of barren dormant trees, skeletal white pines, and thickets of shrubs. This part of the forest was more like what Ben had known from the books Rachel read to him when he was little. Ben caught up with his mom and pressed his shoulder against her. "You can make it up to me by telling what it was like. Before the bears died." Lauren smiled to see them reconnect.

Rachel kissed him. "Thank you for not being mad anymore."

"I hate how everything is different. I wish I'd been born a long time ago."

Rachel sighed, "Me too. But the world has always had problems."

"Yeah, but like this?" He shook his head. "Not like this."

"You're right. Not like this."

North Star

The coughing started a few days before. Everyone noticed, but no one said anything. Worry roiled around in their guts, hoping it was *only* a cough. When Rachel started struggling to breathe and was so tired that the group slowed, Lauren knew that she had to be honest with herself. Their situation was becoming dire. Rachel was sick, and rations were running low.

Lauren fell back to walk beside her sister. "How ya doin'?"

"Not good."

"Do you think it's…?"

"Yes. I need antibiotics."

Lauren dropped her head and sighed. "We think we're only a day or two away from the border. Then maybe another day after that until we find civilization. Do you think you can make it?"

"I don't know. But if anything happens, you have to promise to take care of Ben."

"We're not going to talk like that."

Lauren forced away her dread. Rachel's wracked body faltered, and Lauren grabbed her arm to steady her. Rachel's big brown eyes were filled with alarm, and Lauren felt as if she would fall apart. She picked up a sturdy stick and handed it to Rachel. "This will help you keep your footing."

There was no tool to help Lauren with her emotional balance; she needed to find something from within.

Over the next few days, Rachel's condition worsened, her face flush with fever and obvious confusion. She was barely able to go on. Ben and Khadija were told not to worry. They worried anyway. A sense of doom walked along with them, and Lauren prayed her most fervent prayers that they would cross the border soon. She knew that they were close. The group hiked another few hours that day before they stopped to rest. They slumped their weary selves on a scattering of dark gray covered granite boulders jutting out of the snow. The day's sun was warm and soothing and had melted the icy sheen previously encasing the boulders.

Rachel could barely catch her breath. Lauren ached for her as if she herself were infirm. She was being consumed and tried desperately to cobble together something to cling to, lest she be lost. Gliding around in her consciousness were the words of those who'd helped her understand parts of herself and how to just be during hard times. Lauren took in the surroundings; for all the sadness of the changes to the forest, to the world, there was still beauty. She tried to focus on feeling her sister's presence, rather than feeling her entire being. She looked at the pools of water collected on the ragged surface of the stone. She focused on being there, then. Rosa had talked about how her love for family kept her centered when she had felt like spinning out of control, and yet it was Lauren's affection for Rachel that was the cause of her spinning now. Lauren took in the kids and Erik, collapsed on their own massive boulders.

Her family was beautiful. The slate gray rock upon which they sat was beautiful, with its crevices and bunches of tough lichen that would outlive them all. That rock, born of lava two billion years before was as worn as Lauren felt. She pressed both of her palms against its surface and felt the electric energy of time and space, love and the circle of life weave together. She gazed about the forest and felt calm. The saplings bursting forth into life surrounding them were beautiful, as was the ice in the branches shining in the afternoon light.

These were the places hope lived. Lauren knew that to find peace, she needed to take it moment by moment. Lauren did not want Rachel to die, but she knew that one day she would, as would she and everyone she'd met. What mattered most was the sliver of time before her eyes, not dwelling in the past nor obsessing about a future she couldn't control. She also realized that she had not felt like taking her own life for so long she'd nearly forgotten the urge. She put her head back and closed her eyes, feeling the warmth of the sun on her face. She thought of the rhythms of the earth and the solace and constancy of the moonrises and sunsets. She imagined the stars up in the sky. She breathed in confidence that she would be alright.

Rachel's voice was thin and small when she asked, "What do you say we stop for the night soon, huh?"

When they arrived at that spot to rest, Ben scrambled up onto the tallest of the large boulders, as little boys and others are wont to do. He laid up there until they were ready to go, slowly chewing his chicken jerky. He hopped down onto the smaller rock below and jumped to the ground. He landed with a thud, and the adults winced. He started on his feet, then fell back on his bum, grunting. From beneath him he pulled out the object that poked him as he landed. He found a crumpled rectangular sign and read it. He'd landed on the far side from the others and no one else could see. He held the sign to his chest and marveled at the treasure of his news. He was quiet for so long that Rachel called with as much energy as she had, "Are you alright back there? Let me see you, I'm worried."

He came around the rock with a twinkle in his eye. Holding up the sign so they could see, Ben announced, "No hunting allowed. Quetico Provincial Park."

Everyone looked stunned. Lauren knew what it meant; they all did. But there had been no patrols, no fencing, no drones, no nothing. It was almost unnerving. They'd been prepping for *something*, anything, for a coon's age. Even still, all of them felt a tingling enthusiasm to carry on. They'd made it across the border and were in Kanata.

The bedraggled group swiftly located a giant white pine with long needles clinging on. It formed a canopy from the snow and the needles below were mostly dry and comfortable. At dark Lauren and Erik tucked Rachel and the kids in before hiking a few yards away to a clearing. Lauren pulled out the quadrant she'd made from a protractor and a couple of sticks. She found the Big Dipper and traced its handle down until she located the North Star, enthusiastically guiding lost travelers for millennia with her light. Aligning the instrument and star, Lauren measured the angle.

Erik was looking at the map with the flashlight. "We're about here, I'm thinking. We're probably only half a day or so away from this little nothing of a place called Hilltowne."

"I wonder what we'll find when we get there?" Despite Lauren's insights that night, she was no Zen master and never would be. She fretted, just not as much. Old habits die hard.

"Yeah. Me too."

Rachel's symptoms were far worse by morning, and she carried on with Erik and Lauren carrying her on their backs as much as possible. Lauren could tell that Rachel was embarrassed. She was a proud woman, just like Lauren was. Just like Ann had been, all in their own ways. The glory of crossing the border had faded, but before utter despair set-in, the trees opened up and they stumbled onto a well-maintained paved road. They all rushed toward it with as much zest as they could and wept for joy. They walked along the gravel side of the road for only an hour or so before the sounds of humanity drifted toward them. Car engines and doors slamming could be heard in the distance. Soon a sign appeared, Hilltowne 1 km. Dell's Holler 12 km. Lauren shot Erik and Rachel a smile.

The last bit into town was both the easiest and hardest of their journey, as the hope in their hearts wanted to pull them along faster than their bodies would allow. Within the hour they were on the outskirts of the pocket-sized village. On the main strip there were vehicles of all sorts, from golf carts to a fancy motorcycle parked out around a smattering of businesses. A small square with benches and Kanatian flag gave Lauren some assurance. She crossed her fingers.

A two-story clapboard building hosted both a cafe and hotel sign. Across the way Top 'O the Hill Tavern spilled music onto the sidewalk. Lauren felt as if she was transported back to a tiny town she'd visit from her childhood, like Wykoff or Nerstrand. The party headed straight for the hotel to get Rachel into a bed.

When they opened the door of the hotel, lingering smells of magnificence from the cafe's lunch service brought vicious growls to their stomachs. The two spaces were completely open to each other, with only dimmed lights and changes in floor covering to signal the different rooms. There were two people behind the counter busying themselves with restaurant things. Lauren couldn't *not* read an enormous rough sawn sigh against the wall that read, *"I took a walk in the woods and came out taller than the trees." Thoreau.* A long sturdy branched tree was etched into the spaces around the words and dominated the compact space.

Ben and Khadija were beside themselves with intrigue at the experience of arriving there. Lauren thought it must have been for them like being transported into a different world. Khadija had never been to a town, let alone a restaurant. Ben could only remember driving by collections of buildings, not so much going inside. Rachel didn't take him out unless she had to. Lauren could see the relief on her sister's face. Rachel had told Lauren the day before that she was angry with herself for being sick, and that not being able to care for Ben was like being dead already. Lauren had tried to console her, but Rachel had shriveled inside herself.

The proprietress of the establishment was Georgia, who wore her glasses on her head and a fake smile. She looked up to see their bedraggled crew, put her glasses on and discarded the smile. "Look what the cat's dragged in here, now," she said and rolled her eyes to Ralph, her husband and fellow proprietor of the place.

Erik croaked, "Can we get food, and we need a few rooms? We've got money." Rachel had exchanged thousands of US dollars into Kanatian dollars in anticipation many years before.

Georgia sneered. "How 'bout I see this money first?"

Lauren fished out the money. "Here. This enough for you? Can't you see my sister is sick?" She was offended.

Georgia barbed, "That worries me, too. What's wrong with her? I don't need you bringing anything in here."

Erik said, "We're pretty certain that she picked up anthrax from a herd of dead deer we came across. It's not contagious."

"Then how'd she get it!"

Rachel coughed, "Hi. I'm a person. My name is Rachel and the reason it's not contagious from me to you is because it's only transmitted from dead things to living things. I'm still alive, as you can see. It's called science."

Rachel had been a medical librarian at the Clinic and taken part in the worldwide marches for scientific advancement before the President consolidated power. He threw the country back into the dark ages by firing scientists, dismantling agencies, and falsifying government data. Nothing that came out of Washington could be trusted in the least, which had a corrosive effect around the world. Americans had never understood how much its example of a peaceful transition of power was a beacon across the globe. When the light of U.S. democracy dimmed, authoritarianism and repression marched on in governments around the world.

Georgia inspected the wad of bills. "Fine. Business has been slow, and kids are about the only people I can stand. The cafe's closed, but I can make you up some rooms. How many do you need?"

Erik said, "I don't think you understand, we haven't eaten a real meal in weeks. We're near starved."

Georgia crossed her arms, "I don't think *you* understand. I said we're closed."

Ben broke down, "Pleeeeeasse, lady. I can smell whatever you have, and I will not sleep. I will lay there and cry. Please."

Ralph spoke up, "I've got a pot half-full of soup I can get you. It's still hot. Georgia, can you stop?"

Georgia made a face behind his back. "Fine. More dishes to wash. Won-der-ful!" She was all pinched rudeness. "How many rooms do you want? I got the doll room, the train one, hum... the teddy bear one, too. Three enough?"

Lauren furrowed her brow at the absurdity of the question after what they'd been through. "We'll just take two, I guess. Not the doll one, okay? The others."

Ralph came back within a beat carrying an overflowing basket of bread with dishes of butter and small knives. As they gobbled it up, Ralph said, "Don't mind her. You folks look like you've been through a thing or two."

Erik grabbed the last slice of bread and asked, "Can we get another?"

Lauren tore off bits smothered in melted butter for Rachel. It was the most delicious thing Lauren had ever eaten in her life, but Rachel could hardly swallow. Lauren soaked a cloth in water from her cup and placed it on Rachel's forehead and smoothed the curly wisps of hair around her face. It had gotten tangled and full of knots. She kissed her sister and didn't let herself cry. In a beat Ralph and a teen girl wearing yellow shoes brought in steaming bowls of soup. Lauren slurped and chewed as quickly as she could and had Erik feed Rachel broth while she took off to find the doctor. She went up to the counter and asked Ralph, "Is there a medical clinic or anything around?"

He pointed to the Top o' the Hill. Lauren whimpered. She was anxious as she charged across the plowed lot to get to the bar. She opened the door and a lonely singer crooned out from the radio. It was as seedy a bar as Lauren had ever seen. Mud caked the floor and a lightbulb flickered in the corner. A few dozen patrons filled the stools, and the doctor was the loudest and drunkest among them. Someone pointed him out and Lauren approached. "My sister is sick. I hear you're the doctor."

He guffawed and slapped his knee. "That's what they say, huh? Well, I fancy they're right." He drained his beer.

"She needs antibiotics."

The doctor mused, "Antibiotics, huh? What's wrong with her?"

"We aren't certain, but we think it's anthrax."

He yelled so loud others in the bar stared. "Anthrax! Well why didn't you say that. Yes, you need to get her some antibiotics right away." He signaled the bartender for another beer. Lauren was ready to yank him off the stool by the collar of his flannel shirt.

"Can we go, then?"

"Go where?"

Lauren's face turned red. "To get the antibiotics."

"Oh, oh, yes. I don't have what she needs. I'll need to put in an order. I should get it in a few days. I've been seeing so many cases, I can't keep 'em in stock."

"Can you at least come examine her?" Lauren said with exasperation.

"Sure, I can. Sure, sure. Just let me finish this drink. Where is she?"

Lauren waited while she saw him plug the order for the medicine into his cellphone and went back to the hotel waving her hands around and swearing. She was certain that Rachel wouldn't last and had zero confidence in that fool. She thought of Marium, and what a good care provider she'd been. Lauren felt a twinge of guilt at how she'd initially misjudged her and so many others. The doctor staggered over a few hours later and fudged his way through the exam. He belched and said, "I think you're right." He dug around in his pocket and pulled out a couple of pills. Here's something for her pain. Can I get your number, to let you know when the antibiotics come in?" He winked slow and limp.

Lauren hadn't used a phone to call forever. They used the ham radios at the Resistance camp, but she had music and could sometimes pick up a scattered signal. She said, "I don't have a number and all that."

"Oh, I can set you up in a jiff. You know, I sense you're American. You've got the scent of desperation about you."

Lauren needed the medicine, so she didn't want to piss off the only lifeline she had at the moment. You can fuck all the way off, you drunken prick, she thought. But she said, "Can you just call the room please?"

"What's this one? Teddyville? The other one Traintown? I feel sorry for you with this stupid shit."

Lauren swore, but coming from a doctor it seemed off-putting? But he was quite drunk, which was even more off-putting.

When he left, Lauren murmured, "I'm sorry about him. He's the only doctor they've got."

Rachel whispered, "Both those kids will need you."

Inside Lauren's mind a bullhorn went off; she did not want to be a mom. She wanted to be an auntie. She felt selfish and weak. She tried to will it away but couldn't and wanted to run. She soothed herself by soothing her sister. "You'll be okay. You will. Let's just get some sleep."

Lauren was surprised, as so many years and hurts had passed between them, Lauren didn't think it was possible to love her so thoroughly as she did in that moment. She climbed in bed and folded into her sister like she'd done when she was little. Vivid dreams and nightmares stuck with her each snatch of time she was able to sleep. One such dream was of Rachel sitting on that same rock where the girl had been sitting in her dream all those years before. Rachel's face was warm and bright. Lauren asked, "Why are you so happy?"

"I'm taller than the trees now, Lauren." Then she was gone.

Lauren sat up in horror to see Rachel's face frozen and lifeless.

"No. No. No. Rachel..."

Grief swelled like a tsunami, crushing her and dragging her out to sea. Lauren buried her face in the pillow and screamed and screamed until her throat was raw.

"I don't know if I can do this without you," she sobbed. "But I will try. I will try to get those kids to Nacia with everything I have."

She laid her check against Rachel's back and hoped she was strong enough for what she was now called to do.

James and Ruby - Laws

Ruby and James Abbott were the vision and driving force behind Nacia and its sister city Medeina, but the road getting there was long and winding. Their story was one of desperation and hope in a world gone mad.

The younger of the couple, Ruby Terrell, grew up in Jackson, Mississippi and went off to Tulane University when she had just turned seventeen. Ruby's mother had homeschooled her and her brother because the school system in Jackson wasn't what she and her husband would have called *acceptable*. They were parents with stern expectations of excellence for their children. Ruby's mother did most of the teaching, and she was preparing her children for the world as it was, rather than one that she wished it were. Ruby's mom knew that her kids would have to work twice as hard to get half the credit. It made Ruby strong, without making her hard. Even in the midst of those dismal conditions, her Ruby sparkled.

Ruby's mom hadn't been ready to let her go, even though she'd long since run out of materials to teach. Her spirited daughter was bursting out of the seams of their stifling town, and Ruby had her sights set on New Orleans, Louisiana. She'd tell her mom, "It's the closest you can get to living outside of the United States as any city in the country. Have you seen the pictures of those buildings with their balconies and flowers? They've got their own vibe, their own rhythm in that city. That's where I want to go, Mama." Ruby's mother eventually relented, despite the city's sometimes questionable reputation. She trusted her daughter. It was close to home, and she figured that it was better than Ruby traipsing off overseas when she was old enough to choose for herself.

Ruby enrolled in Tulane's anthropology program since she'd long been fascinated with human evolution and culture. She earned high marks and got involved in just about every group on campus. Ruby knew that she was blessed to have her parents and a scholarship supporting her to give her such freedom, seeing how hard some of her friends worked to pay tuition and keep up with their grades. Ruby was keenly aware of how crushing student debt limited the professional options of so many and appreciated her parent's careful planning to give her and her brother that freedom. Of course, Ruby's parents would have preferred a career in medicine or law, but they learned early on that Ruby would only allow them so much directing.

In freshman year Ruby was at a cafe downtown meeting with a few other members of the foreign affairs club when the bell on the door jingled. Ruby glanced up to see a tall drink of water framed by the chipped wood door frame. He flashed a dazzling smile her way, and her heart leaped. Ruby grinned and tapped her pencil on the table as introductions were made all around. James was quiet, but in a thoughtful way. He was funny, with humor not intended to sting.

James came from a very different world than Ruby. He grew up in southern California with a single mom who worked day and night to provide. He was an only child, though he grew up with cousins and many friends. It seemed his mom couldn't catch a break as something was always hitting the fan. They couch surfed sometimes, and an empty belly was no stranger. James's mother dreamed of greatness for her son, nevertheless. James was the name of five presidents and that was the name her son would have. She tutored him at nights and on weekends and tolerated little bullshit. James outstripped his peers by far and earned a prestigious scholarship to study engineering at Tulane. His goal was to mold the profession toward addressing systemic inequalities in the built environment, of which there were many.

After just a year of dating, Ruby and James made their parents exceedingly unhappy when they eloped. Neither mother approved, since they were still quite young. Ruby said, "I love him. And when you know it's right, you just know."

Of course, at the time Ruby had not understood that love was only a word. It was commitment that turned out to be what mattered. She and James remained with each other long past the time that the marriage was breezy and fun. They made vows that they took more seriously than many. Their marriage, like the rest of life, had seasons. Some of those times were just as light and joyous as when they were young, and other times felt near impossible to move forward together. Through it all they tried to remember that they were each other's best friends.

Ruby and James promised their parents to at least wait to have kids, which was easy since neither wanted them yet. They stayed in New Orleans after Ruby graduated with a Master's, and she went to work for a refugee resettlement project. James was finishing a grueling PhD program and wanted to go into teaching. Six years into their marriage, Ruby gave birth to a little girl, Pearl, who was just three when Hurricane Katrina bore down on their city. Her little brother Antonne was newborn, and Ruby was still nursing. James had a vasectomy after their second child. Two was enough. Two was perfect, they believed. Like many city people, they didn't own a car to leave when the hurricane headed their way. They had two kitties and only about two hundred dollars in cash, so paying for rental cars and hotels was out of the question. Their parents were frantic for them to leave and wired money. But one thing after another fell through and they were trapped in the city. Their apartment was on the ground floor situated near a levee more fragile than almost anyone knew. They planned to go to the roof if water started to rise. When Katrina's eye shifted away slightly, and her speed diminished, they went to bed thinking they'd dodged a bullet.

The next morning, the news was dominated by news of levee breaches as Lake Pontchartrain began filling the streets. Clear information about what to do was nonexistent. Rescue services were nowhere to be seen. Neighbors begin hiking through the waters to get to safety. James wanted to join them, but Ruby insisted on waiting for a boat. She'd lived through flooding in Jackson and knew the dangers all too well. The family made their way to the second-floor stairwell and hoped that help would arrive. In the aftermath of the disaster, local, state, and federal responses became poster children of ineptitude. The Abbott's hope rose when they heard the roar of a boat engine at long last. James hung out the window with a sheet. A wizened creole fisherman called out "How many ya'll got in there?"

"Four of us. Two adults, a baby and a toddler."

"Alrighty, brah. Climb on out of that window and onto the roof ledge. We can ease you down."

Ruby set Antonne down and James helped her onto the ledge. She dangled down into their flat boat with the help of the fisherman's son. The fisherman said, "Sit on down, miss. My boy will get the little boo." Ruby reluctantly agreed and sat on the bench.

"I've got 'im!" he said and handed the child to Ruby. Ruby held Antonne close as he wailed.

James looked at Pearl and instructed, "You're next. He's going to help you down like he did with mommy." Pearl shrieked and wrapped her arms around her father's neck. James realized that he'd have to climb out with her and stepped onto the slippery roof. The fisherman's son was trying to get Pearl into his arms, but she howled and held tighter.

Ruby cried, "Please, baby. Go to the nice man. He's here to help us!"

The more they begged, the more Pearl struggled. Antonne's face was red and his bawls echoed out across the flooded neighborhood. James slipped then regained his footing. Everyone gasped, watching helplessly as his other foot gave way. James and Pearl splashed into the flooded yard below. When he surfaced, Pearl still had her grip. But the current was swift, and they became tangled in a row of dense bushes. James was thrashing to free them and did not feel his little girl's hands slip away.

Pearl screamed as the fisherman tried to bring the boat closer. The current pulled Pearl away as she fought to stay alive. "Daddy, Mommy, help me!" Ruby nearly dove in after her, but the fisherman's son caught hold of her. Ruby wailed and fought against him. James was only able to stay above water as he watched his baby dragged away by the forces of nature. Her mangled body was found days later in a culvert. Ruby and James were changed, as only someone who's lost a child could understand.

Their marriage suffered as they blamed each other for their daughter's death, in ways big and small. In equal parts they blamed themselves. Once they worked through that pain, they were left with the realization that Pearl didn't die because James slipped. She died because the whole world had slipped. Systems upon systems failed them. Failed Pearl. And ultimately, were failing everyone. They channeled their grief into the singular focus of righting the wrongs that had led to their daughter's death. They fully understood that most tragedies weren't simply what happened in a discrete moment but were the result of fermentation and froth that created the space for it to occur. The Abbotts were determined to smash the systems that led to their child's death and build a world that didn't sweep babies away.

James and Ruby came into the fight after years in the trenches of activism, though Katrina sharpened their focus. The monstrous size of the storm was unprecedented; the hot oceans and air that fueled Katrina were an undeniable fact. But racial and economic injustices were as responsible for the surge, failed levees, and ensuing chaos as the storm itself. As they searched for answers, the depths of the rabbit holes of causality and their network of shadowy tunnels sent James and Ruby into emotional turmoil. The entire system was broken, and they asked themselves which threads needed pulling first.

As they understood it, the same culprit emerged over and again – the oil and gas industry that had trampled on Louisiana and the rest of the world. They built channels through swamps that should have blunted the hurricane's storm surge. The companies created the paths to access their oil rigs that extracted oil from deep beneath the ocean's floor. The oil that when burned released the carbon that gave the Earth a fever and drove devilish storms. Aside from burning humanity alive, perhaps these companies' greatest sins were the creation of a culture of impunity, where failed public servants were told they'd done *one hell of a job*, and politicians claimed missions accomplished that weren't and took *no responsibility at all* for what transpired on their watch.

Katrina opened the eyes of many to long simmering problems, but to James and Ruby it opened a whole world of crazy. When they'd put all the pieces together, people would look at them like they'd lost their minds. The couple had done their research, though, and were undeterred. James finished his PhD and went to work for a department at Tulane. Ruby homeschooled their son, just as she had been, and took to activism full time as Antonne trotted along with her to meetings. Ruby fretted that he was behind other kids his age and that the cause was the contaminated FEMA trailer they ended up in briefly after the storm. He'd been sickly since. Their daughter Pearl was never far from their minds, though they were able to find a different sort of contentment again. They went back to New Orleans to help rebuild and settled into a little apartment off Esplanade, this time on the top floor. Ruby finally got her balcony with crimson flowers, and they found their new normal. Or so they thought.

One day, Ruby was at her desk working on a proposal to fund her next project. She said to James and Antonne, "Bother me at your peril, gentlemen." They were smart, so they gave her a wide berth. Antonne played in his room, and James went to check the mail. He opened the silver metal box and pulled out the usual stack of bills and ads. Tucked in the middle was a thick paper envelope with gold lettering addressed to him.

He grabbed the railing and settled down on the stoop. Reading over the letter again and calling out loudly,

"Ruby! Ruby! Get out here!" A disheveled and annoyed Ruby appeared on the balcony.

"What in God's name?"

"Get down here!"

When she came he handed her the paper. She read it and said, "Your mother had been telling the truth about who your father was. James do you know what this means?"

"Yes, it means everything changes."

James's father was a South African billionaire who'd made a fortune in the telecommunications industry. James didn't know that his father had been following his life behind the scenes for years. His *legitimate* sons had died, and James was the sole heir.

The money came at first as a great shock to James, Ruby and Antonne. Many who they'd thought were friends drifted away, no matter how hard they all tried to keep things as they were. Others who were clearly not friends tried to cling on. The entire situation was overwhelming for the family. Though for a family who'd lived their lives paycheck to paycheck, this money brought opportunity like they'd never known. Quickly, the burden set in however as they learned the rotten legacy of James's father's business. They decided to use half the money to help the people of South Africa and turn the rest toward the causes into which they'd already invested their lives.

The family laid out priorities and funded whatever they could. Some days felt like wins, others not-so-much. Their focus was on what they could accomplish each day, rather than thinking too much on the frightening big picture. For that picture could feel hopeless at times. When they wanted to curl up in bed and never get up again, they remembered this mantra. The devastation of COVID on their beloved city was almost as bad as Katrina. James and Ruby's new foundation gave grants to the city and others across the country and the world to address threat multipliers that made every problem worse.

Many places were making progress on climate adaptation and justice relative to others. With their successes, James and Ruby were coming to national prominence. They were among the most effective advocates for big structural changes that could address numerous challenges simultaneously. They were also outspoken critics of the rise of authoritarian regimes across the globe. Like George Soros, the Party needed a scapegoat and found James and Ruby to fit the bill nicely. The President's press lied and ran them down. They had to hire a security team because threats were flooding in. But after the President's second and unending term began, the menace came from the government itself. Their security teams would be no use against the FBI.

James and Ruby both agreed that it was time to leave the United States. Due to their wealth and influence, many countries were eager to play host. Russia, China and Iran all extended invitations hoping to humiliate America on the international stage even more than she'd humiliated herself. One dictator was the equivalent of another to James and Ruby, though, since one's fortune or downfall rested on their whims alone. Democratic countries alone were being considered, but Ruby worried about the rise of the far right across Europe. Not content to simply move themselves and their lives, they wanted to create something more. When she proposed Nacia, Ruby said it was visionary. James said it was insane. Ruby knew that he was right, but that she was right too.

She wanted to build something brand new that she hoped to be a demonstration city. Ruby said that they could try out materials, techniques and policies that could be used elsewhere. Ruby wanted to be as far away from the rest of civilization as she could. James was more reluctant, saying, "Running away won't solve anything. No one is safe until we're all safe." James was more introspective and took more time to come to a decision than Ruby.

"I'm not saying we give up the work and hide," Ruby said. "We redouble the work, but we also invest in somewhere that can withstand just about anything that comes along. This is what I need for our son, and I'm not going to apologize for wanting somewhere safe for him. We've already lost one child, James. I cannot lose another."

James could not argue with her, and Nacia was born. He never regretted it.

Ruby was the public face of their monumental fundraising efforts for Nacia and other adaptive projects for existing cities. After one of her popular speeches, Ruby was often approached by throngs of people wanting to talk, often by crying white women wanting to tell her how inspiring she was. Ruby tried to be civil, but tired quickly of their fragility. Others would approach her and brag on their million-dollar doomsday bunkers. Still more might approach her after they've had a few drinks at the reception and embarrassingly admit to such a hideaway for themselves. Ruby could understand the desire to lock one's self and children away from the pain. There was a certain posh appeal to the concept of riding-out the end of the world in style. Though the very idea of being underground in one of these bunkers gave Ruby the creeps - like already being buried in a grave. She'd always heard people talk about their burial plots with engraved names in stone for *when the time comes*. It was the same language people used about their luxury burrows.

Ruby liked to joke privately, "These bunker people just bought a chit to the gloom of Hades, is what they've done. And I'll bet they didn't even get a persimmon." Ruby was a forthright intense woman with a sharper intellect and wit than most and a flare for style. She was generally the smartest and most sophisticated person in the room, and James remained in awe of her throughout their lives. While Ruby objected to doomsday bunkers on principle, James was more circumspect from an engineering standpoint. "They're not being built by people with a demonstrated interest in the survival of anyone. History is littered with technological marvels that failed - planes that fell out of the sky and bridges that collapsed. The people building these bunkers have no more concern for these saps who'll live below ground than the bodies they've left above ground."

Ruby tried to get donors to see the big picture. As a girl, she and her friends had a mad crush on the young handsome preacher at their church. Ruby channeled his tone and mannerisms when she gave an address. She was a sought-after speaker and would approach the podium to thunderous applause.

"We're here, friends, to talk about big things! We are here to talk about innovation! We are here to talk about Nacia! And we are here for you to get out your checkbooks." The audience would laugh. "We're living in an unprecedented era of human history. Experiencing changes never seen since humanity emerged on this Earth. And we need solutions equal to these challenges. What we're trying to do with Nacia is create somewhere that can endure and adapt. We're not thinking of this experiment as merely some sort of escape from the problems of the world...But to integrate with the world in a whole new way. We're creating a model for progressive democratic rule where we can integrate what we've long known about how people live and work best. We're working to integrate the best of our scientific and engineering know-how to address complex problems before us. And we need to bring technology into our lives in a way that brings us together instead of pulling us apart. All these things I say now are probably not too controversial. Too strange. Right? But dare I say that there are two more ways we need to integrate that you might not be so keen on." The audience would usually chuckle nervously, unsure what to expect.

"Friends, we need to integrate love and equality into our lives. And not just love for those near to us, but we need to extend our circle of concern to include everyone. We know we do. We have to. No one is safe until everyone is safe. And I'm not talking about some flat concept of equality that assumes we're all the same. Nor am I talking about one that assumes we're all too different and should stay separate. We tried that once. Am I right, folks?" A few in the crowd would understand her reference. Ruby would point to them and say, "Alright, you got that. Good. We have to figure out ways to coexist that don't tear each other apart.

Now, let me throw one more thing at you. There's another thing - a monumental thing - that we need to bring this whole thing together. We need to integrate with nature, too. There's no two ways about it. Let's face it, we've been spending the better part of this last dozen or so thousand years trying to bend Gia - our Earth - toward what we want. That's the human condition, to some extent. Right? But we have to understand that the Earth will go on with or without us. The Earth will go on whether we're happy and fed or cold and miserable. All systems have a breaking point, and this interconnected web of life we rely on is reaching the point of no return.

Humanity is as subject to physics, chemistry, and biology as any creature on this planet! These are laws above the laws of men. These are the laws of nature. And we are as in need of paying attention to these as you all should be to the laws of securities fraud. But, I'm here today to tell you that it's this fantastical thinking that humans are so unique and separate, somehow above it all, that's much of what's gotten us into this mess in the first place." Ruby never got past bracing for this next portion of the speech. "I do not mean to cause offense to you lovely and so, so generous people! But you are the very folks who need to be taking this message in. Those of you who are living comfortable lives still, who think you're insulated because of your wealth and power from the chaos that's enveloping our planet - you need to hear me. You, personally, and your families are subject to these same laws. And it's happening today. Right now. Not in our children's children's generation. But in our generation. The planet we need to survive is changing in ways that you may not be able to envision. And most of it seems far away and nebulous to you. I know. I hear you."

Ruby would get the audience involved to keep their attention, which was why she drew a packed crowd, despite the topic being sullen. She'd ask a list of questions and for a show of hands for anyone who could say yes to one of them. "Don't believe me that climate change is here now? Let me prove it. Who here has been or knows someone who's been affected by an unexpected or usual flood? Okay, keep your hands up. If you can say yes to another, put your other hand up. If you get to three, stand up. Now, show me if you've dealt with wildfires outside of what used to be wildfire season? Record-setting heat wave? Arctic cold snap? Drought? Major hurricane? Massive tornado? Derecho?" She'd go on until nearly everyone was standing. "Look around you. This is the face of climate change."

Ruby's voice mixed somber with sarcasm for her close. "You can't fight chemistry, folks. The air is different now than it was. Call it the atmosphere if you like. But that tiny bubble we're breathing is filling up with carbon and methane and other gases that we're putting up there, and it's holding in too much heat. You can argue as much as you want that this isn't true. But the evidence is there, and it's been there for a long time. It used to not even be controversial if you can believe that. Even the Party knew it was real. Because these are the laws of nature, folks. Science doesn't care if you believe it. Science doesn't care about your feelings. If you have a problem with the science, you don't have a problem with me. You've got a problem with the forces natural or supernatural that made those laws. Humanity cannot change them! No matter how much power or technology we have. Whether you write me a check today isn't what matters. Though, of course you should do that. What matters is what all of us can do to make a difference. Many people ask me if I think people will go extinct...No one can know the answer to that, least alone me. But I also reject the question. I do. Because I find it unproductive. For me, the real question is *how* will humanity survive? Will we implement the solutions that we already know and vigorously pursue new answers? Or will we allow a slow descent to chaos? We know in our bones that things are bad. Actually, the very best question is, what are you going to do to make it better?"

Medeina

The boat made few ripples in the water as it chugged its way toward land. Bursts of fluffy clouds dotted the sky in the warm afternoon sun. Lauren could almost have thrown herself out of the boat and let the lake water take her far away. Since Rachel's death, she was responsible for two souls aside from her own – Ben and Khadija – and she was not at all sure she was handling it well. The kids had been beside themselves since Rachel passed, and Lauren felt scarcely capable of managing her own grief, let alone theirs. She was so grateful for Erik. He'd held them, soothed them, and provided a sense of stability. Lauren loved him more than ever.

When Lauren discovered Rachel died, she called the doctor. He'd come over a short while later wearing the same clothes from the night before, eyes red and filled with sleep. He offered little in the way of compassion or competence, but he did offer something else. "I can arrange transport to Nacia. I have a few connections there, too. I can get you set up."

Lauren wondered if this was real since he seemed like such a slickster and kept hitting on her. But Lauren asked Ralph about him, and he said that he was the only one in town carrying people to and from Nacia. So, Erik and Lauren reluctantly agreed to pay his excessive fees to get to the lake near Nacia to ferry across.

The boat conductor dropped Erik, Lauren, Ben, and Khadija on the dock then he pointed his flat-bottomed boat in the direction from which they'd come and piloted away without a word. There were a handful of watercraft lying on the beach and two brick buildings on shore. One of the buildings had a sign that read, "Welcome New Residents."

Lauren said, "I guess we're in the right place." In the building was a woman wearing a crisp uniform with a name tag informing all that her name was Doris. She was pleasant but spoke quickly. She handed Lauren a stack of pamphlets and a tablet to fill out their information. Lauren wasn't registering everything she was saying until she heard the words *second city* and *tent*.

Lauren remarked, "Wait a second. We're here to get to Nacia."

A hint of sadness passed over Doris's eyes. "Sweetie, you know Nacia is full, right? I'm directing you to the sister city that's being built called Medeina. They'll help you get set up over there. I guess the doctor didn't tell you?"

Lauren put her fingers through her hair. "No, he didn't. You've got to be kidding me. What is the other city like?"

Doris's eyes were all the way sad this time, as she glanced at the kids. "It's fine, but... You know, compared to a lot of places in this world. You'll be okay. Keep them close."

Rachel would have been so disappointed. Lauren was glad she was spared this, at least. Rachel had believed in her dream so strongly. Lauren hadn't known what to expect, but not this. They had been in Hilltowne for three days and no one had mentioned that Nacia was full. The Doctor was evasive whenever Lauren asked anything. He always turned it into some cocky sex joke at her expense. She hated him, and now this. She'd learned to trust her gut on the scavenger teams and was pissed at herself for not being more prepared.

Doris gave them a map of the interior of the new city and smiled, "Good luck! Stop and say hi if you ever want to talk. I'm here all the time, even though it's just one or two people usually coming through." Lauren was relieved that they were at least being taken care of and welcomed but was apprehensive. She presumed that the kids had overheard but hadn't checked in with them about how they were doing. In fact, she'd barely spoken with them or made eye contact since Rachel died. Lauren knew that she was coming across as cold and distant like her mom, Ann, but couldn't seem to stop herself. Lauren wondered if Ann had been so distant for the same reasons.

Nacia was built about twenty years before and sat less than a mile from the new city of Medeina. James and Ruby had seen the need for another city as conditions in the world grew worse. They knew eventually refugees would be on their doorstep, and they wanted to be prepared. But they'd built only the exterior walls and basic power and water infrastructure. It was like the fields of hundreds of football stadiums together, with no seats against the walls and various internal temporary structures. Ruby and James wanted the city's new residents to mold and shape their community as they saw fit, but hadn't anticipated the lack of leadership for the effort. In the two years since people had been arriving, only one person had stepped in to take charge, and that wasn't going well.

Lauren and the others rounded a stone path and before them lay the new city. The entrance was one massive archway framed by oversize tiles. There was a vast plaza extending between the inside and outside of the city with dormant deciduous trees surrounding the sides. People gathered in clumps and few seemed friendly.

Lauren spoke to Erik quietly so the children wouldn't hear. "I'm not getting the best vibe. Why didn't anyone tell us about two cities?"

"No kidding. That doctor was so sketchy."

"As fuck. Do you think we should do anything different?"

Erik groaned, "Let's give this place a shot first. We're all ragged."

When they got inside, Khadija held up the map. "It looks like over there is where we get the tents and that way to get food."

Ben whined, "Where do we sleep?"

Khadija whined back. "Straight ahead, I guess. It looks like half the place is under construction."

Lauren whispered to Erik, "I don't know if I can handle these kids."

They were headed over to the building for their supplies when Lauren heard her name shouted. She whipped around to see someone running to her. "Pedro!" Lauren grabbed him and hugged him with all her might. "I thought you'd died!"

"I thought you had, too. It's so good to see you. I've got to go, but I'll come find you later…" He took off as suddenly as he appeared. Lauren couldn't stop smiling at seeing him again.

They picked up a blue tent identical to the others filling the interior of the city and made their way to the far side where new encampments were being set up. Lauren noticed the kids were particularly quiet, but she was appreciating time to her own thoughts. She startled when she noticed Ben glaring at her. She asked, "What?"

"We heard you."

"Heard what?"

Khadija chimed in. "We heard that you didn't want us."

"That's not what I said." Lauren was shocked.

Erik said, "She just meant things are hard is all."

Ben crossed his arms. "That's not what she meant, and you know it. You're both liars."

Lauren's head swirled. "I'm sorry I hurt your feelings. It's just hard. I love you both, but I don't know if I can ever do as good of a job as your mothers did, and that scares me."

Khadija responded, "Well, you have to want to try first."

Lauren could see the hurt in their faces and felt ashamed. She was failing them already. She continued working, but before long Pedro found them again. He'd brought his wife and nephew, too, and the reunion brought everyone joy. They exchanged stories of harrowing tales about escaping the camp and the news of the deaths. Lauren asked how long they'd been at Medeina, and Pedro surprised her when he said weeks.

"How'd you get here so fast?"

Pedro had a sly smile. "Let's just say we borrowed one of the government's trucks."

Pedro's wife suggested taking the kids off her hands. The kids were still angry and readily agreed. Lauren breathed a sigh of relief. Erik said, "See, we're not trying to do this alone." Lauren nodded.

After they'd gone, Pedro vented. "This place is a wreck. I can't even figure out what's going on. Did you see that they're organizing an election for a co-presidency? Me and you did a bang-up job at the Camp. I think we'd make a great team."

Lauren was incredulous. "Me? President? No thanks. That's not something I could do."

"You certainly could! Who better than a farm girl from Minnesota and a scientist from Honduras to save a city in Kanata?" He laughed. "We'd be a hell of a lot better than the Doctor. He's the only one who's running right now."

Lauren looked puzzled. "Hold up. The Doctor? Drunk all the time, wears a dirty flannel?"

"That's the one. I'm nearly certain he's been stealing supplies and selling them. Plus, I've heard bad rumors."

"What rumors?" Her eyes narrowed.

"There's a couple guys working for him who've been preying on some of the kids who are here alone. They say they're doing terrible things."

Lauren thought about the garotte in her pocket and started pacing. "Where is he? I think I should have a word with him."

Erik said, "Let's think this through," but Lauren was already off. She was shouting, and people were staring. Erik pulled her behind the wall of one of the construction zones for privacy. Lauren's voice echoed in the empty space. "I hate him and everyone like him. I hate Bryan! I hate Eric!" Lauren had never spoken her attacker's name aloud to her husband. She was crumbling and had no strength to stop it. She began sobbing uncontrollably.

Erik was confused. "You hate me?"

Lauren mumbled inaudibly. "No, not you."

"I'm sorry. I can't hear you."

Lauren yelled, her face red and furious. "My rapist's name was Eric! Okay!"

He finally understood.

"I'm sorry, Laur. Come here, I'll take care of you."

He went to embrace her, but Lauren pushed him away. "Don't say that!"

"What?"

"That you'll take care of me. It scares me." Tendrils of the deepest pain lurking in her began unfurling. She was grasping to remain steady as the tears poured out.

Erik's eyes were sad. "I don't understand why that would scare you."

"Because I don't deserve it, Erik. I don't deserve to be taken care of. Look at how I've been treating you and the kids. Look at everything I've done!" She slumped down on a stack of plywood sheeting. Erik sat next to her and let her cry until she was wrung out.

"Of course you deserve to be cared for, Lauren. Everyone does. You're holding all of us together, and you don't even realize it. We need you, honey. We all do." They sat quietly for a good while before Erik added, "No wonder you've never said that name. I'm sure I remind you of him every day."

Erik wiped the tears from her cheek, and she let him pull her in. She whispered, "You're nothing like him. You're sweet and gentle. You see me. He saw right through me." She felt her heart swell for him and wash away her agony.

She'd never known such abandon as she shoved away lust's guilt and her long simmering shame. Lauren purred into Erik's ear *I love you* as she accepted his flesh into her own. She was experiencing a surge of perfect contentment and fell back in exhaustion after. She was grinning like a Cheshire cat, more fully alive, more fully herself than ever. It wasn't the sex per se, as the allowing herself to integrate everything she was - her wildness, her vulnerability, and her strength. She felt that she could be all those things at the same time. As she laid in Erik's arms, she knew what she needed to do.

Erik and Lauren went to collect the kids from Pedro and were giggling like teenagers. When Lauren saw Ben and Khadija, she apologized profusely, hugged them, kissed them, and told them, "Never doubt how committed I am to you or how much I love you." All was forgiven. Then Lauren turned to Pedro, "You still up for running for the Presidency?"

Pedro picked her up and spun her around. "Yes, indeed."

Pedro and Lauren dove headfirst into their wild venture. They first learned about the official process for beginning their candidacy and arranged for conference calls with low-level officials at Nacia who were helping with the election. They began reading the official constitution of Nacia and Medeina, which was based on principles laid out by Abdullah Öcalan, a Kurdish philosopher. He described his political philosophy as democratic confederalism, which consisted of autonomy, direct democracy, a sharing economy and respect for all cultures, the environment and women's rights. The new city would be run by two co-equal presidents.

Lauren's primary concern at the moment was with security. Based on Öcalan's work, they created a group called the Mamas, which was composed entirely of women who handled most of the conflicts among residents. Almost immediately, the citizens were feeling more secure. From his base in Hilltowne, the Doctor watched all this happening and was beginning to feel threatened. He became incensed, however, when he realized that they had also begun patrolling warehouses to reduce losses and were inventorying shipments as they came in. Neither one had seen the other since Hilltowne, but the Doctor decided that he needed to pay Lauren a visit.

He caught up with her one afternoon while she was on patrol. "Hey, Lauren. Remember me?"

She frowned. "How could I forget?"

"I heard you and that beaner are running for office. That's pretty foolish. I wouldn't want anything bad happening to that sweet face of yours." He smirked.

Lauren stared him square in the eyes. "My partner's name is Pedro, actually. And yes, we are running because I'm tired of corrupt fools like you."

"Corrupt? Fool? Those are some harsh words. You need to back down, or you'll come to regret it."

Lauren was worried but didn't let it show. She and Pedro agreed to stay the course but knew that they needed help. Through the officials they'd already been in touch with, Lauren arranged for an in-person meeting with James and Ruby at Nacia. A sinewy man named Minato met them at the entrance and took them on a tour of before their meeting. They walked down a large central hall to an ornately carved wooden door, and when Minato opened it, Lauren's breath caught. Warm moist air filled with the smell of freshly turned earth spilled over them. A large clear dome covered a vast courtyard teeming with activity. Though it was winter outside, inside the trees were tall and leafed out. Branches of red and gold raspberries hung heavy. Purple and pink flowers sprinkled color through the scene. A group of children tossed a ball in a grassy area next to a playground. A dozen chickens pecked at the soil near them and a pen of goats bleated off to the side. Earthen paths wound through the space, with benches and sculptures scattered about. "It's gorgeous!" Lauren declared.

A pair of golden retrievers wagged over. Minato said, "This is Charlie and Buddy. They live here in the courtyard. They're everyone's dogs, but they have their favorite humans."

Lauren bent down and hugged Charlie. The dog licked her face. "Who's the best boy?" She'd forgotten how much she missed animals.

Minato also showed them the public buildings off the central plaza, including an art studio, a pub, and a community center. Houses were arranged in long sections radiating out from the middle down rambling passageways. Lauren looked at Pedro with delight. "Could we build something like this?" The tour ended at the administrative building where James and Ruby had offices, and everyone settled around a large conference table to talk.

James started. "We've been paying attention to what you've been up to. We're impressed."

Pedro said, "It hasn't been easy. The Doctor's been a real obstacle. That's why we're here. We're pretty sure he's been stealing supplies, and he threatened Lauren when he found out we were running for office. Of course, you probably know that he's running, too."

Ruby sighed, "Yes, we know all about him. He got here a couple of years ago. He was one of the first ones. He's not even a doctor since he dropped out of medical school. He's a low-level grifter who got his hands on some power and doesn't want to give it up. That's why we're so happy you've thrown your hat in the ring. We felt like we were going to have to cancel the elections if no one else stepped up."

Lauren asked, "How'd things get so bad? I don't understand why you didn't just take charge over there?"

James responded, "We've been helping with security and leadership development. But a place run by outsiders is never going to be as sustainable as when the people take responsibility for their own community. We could go in there and tell everyone how to do things, but we feel like that would just build resentment and could lead to bigger problems in the long-term."

Lauren said, "I can see that. But this Doctor has so much power. What are we going to do about him?"

Ruby answered, "*We* aren't going to do anything. The question is, what are *you* going to do? Here's the thing, it's not like the Doctor waltzed in here showing us his true colors. He came in just like you did, all offers and smiles. Anyone can present themselves as a leader. The question is, what kind of a leader do you want to be?"

Lauren shrugged, "A good one?"

"Right answer. But what kind of a good one? Here's what I've got for you, at the end of the day the best leaders are actually not leaders at all. They're servants because they put people first. They lift those around them; they empower others to greatness. That's what you and Pedro have already started. You keep that up, and there's no way you'll lose.

The only way people would vote for that wretched Doctor is if they're scared. Fear is a powerful emotion. It drives so much more of our behavior than most people realize. We humans think we're so fancy and sophisticated, but in evolutionary terms, we're barely out of the trees. We've got these primal reptile-like brains underneath all that elegant gray matter, and that reptile brain is spirited. It had to be! That's where our fight, flight and freeze is located. That's what kept us safe from danger back when it was lions trying to eat us. The new lions are people like the Doctor who traffic in fear, but our brains don't know how to understand those kinds of threats.

Humans evolved in small groups where everyone was very similar, and all knew every other in their group. With large communities we can't possibly know everyone and people can be so outwardly different from each other that we can forget we're all the same deep down. The Doctor knows this an is exploiting it. He knows that if he can keep people cowering or filled with rage, he'll stay in control. But we have even more powerful motivations than fear, and that's love. You two show the people of Medeina that you're all working together for the same goal and show them that you care about them. They'll trust you. They'll come to love you, and that's how you'll win.

Lauren and Pedro left Nacia with more drive than before. Still, Lauren worried about the kids and Erik. She spoke to him that night. "If I do this, I won't be around much. I'll have so many responsibilities. I feel like I'm always expecting so much from everyone. Like I'm selfish."

Erik assured her, "Having a will doesn't mean you're either selfish or that you're pushy. Through your life people expected you to only exist the way they wanted you to. I know you were close with Rachel, but she had her expectations, too. I want you to be whatever you want to be now. I can take care of myself. And you know I always wanted kids. Let me take care of them. You take care of Medeina." She was overjoyed at his support, even though a bit of guilt lingered.

She and Pedro threw the full force of their energies toward running for office. Since the internet was free and open in Kanata, Lauren arranged to use some of her cash to buy a bevy of cell phones. They took their campaign online; they took their campaign to the floor of Medeina and they took Ruby's call to service seriously. They continued organizing work crews and shoring up internal security. The more successful they were, the more people volunteered to help.

The Doctor continued his campaign as well. He gave speeches denouncing Lauren as "nasty" and Pedro as someone from the "dark shadows." He arranged with hackers to disrupt their campaign's website and gave out false information regarding the election. There were no polls but based on enthusiasm it was obvious who was on track to win.

As election day arrived, Lauren, Pedro and their supporters tried to make sure that everyone over sixteen had cast a ballot. There were three polling places set-up throughout the compound, but the doctor had his people in place intimidating anyone they suspected of voting against them. Lauren was beside herself with worry as the hours ticked by until voting ended. They waited as officials from Nacia counted and then recounted. The Doctor fought abut the numbers and kept dragging out the process for weeks. When election officials were satisfied with the county, they certified the results.

Ruby, James, and the rest of Nacia's governing council called the doctor and his running-mate into the office along with Lauren and Pedro. Ruby beamed. "We have a winner. Well, I guess we have two winners. Pedro, Lauren, congratulations."

The Doctor balled up his fists, "I refuse to accept the results. The election was rigged."

James replied flatly, "You know that's not true. You did every rotten thing to win, and you still lost. Why don't you take your defeat like an adult now?"

"I will not. This is an outrage." The Doctor stormed out and Pedro followed.

In the hall Pedro got directly in his face and dripped with venom. "I need you to hear something and get it into your head now. Okay? I've been playing nice with you, but I'm done. You get the hell away from this city and take your bunch of rapists and thieves with you, or I will personally make sure each of your throats are slit in your sleep."

The Doctor stumbled back. "You're full of shit. Get the fuck away from me."

Pedro stepped forward. "I've slaughtered entire villages of men, women and children, you sonofabitch. You think I can't take you down?"

The doctor's eyes were wild with fear. He left the city and never returned.

Pedro casually walked back into the room. At the time Lauren asked, "What was that all about?"

"Nothing much. I don't think we have to worry about him anymore, though." Pedro later revealed to Lauren his own massive secret. He had been a microbiologist and left Honduras with his nephew, just as he'd told her before he left. This time, he added the details that he was also on the run. Pedro was in charge of a secret biological weapons program for an elite military until and defected when his conscience couldn't take it anymore. Since then he'd become a Buddhist and pacifist, but he knew he could still intimidate when need be. The skill came in handy on sparing occasions during his presidency.

Residents of Medeina and many from Nacia were gathered outside for the announcement of the election results. A tall wooden stage had been erected with the flag of each city on the dais. Erik, Ben, and Khadija sat in chairs along with Pedro's wife and nephew. They were giddy with excitement.

Ruby declared their victory to uproarious cheers. Lauren and Pedro held hands and exchanged looks of awe and terror at their new responsibilities. They decided that Lauren would go first with her speech in English, and Pedro would follow with a delivery in Spanish and then French, covering most of the languages spoken at the camp. Ruby loaned Lauren a stunning red dress with gold embroidered flowers for the occasion.

Lauren's mouth was dry and her palms sweaty as she approached the microphone. The audience was chanting her name, and she felt like she was in a dream. She looked over at her family, brimming with pride. She thought of those she'd lost, and how surprised Rachel would be if she could see her now. Lauren wasn't sure she was up for this job. But she was sure that she would give it everything she had as she began.

"Thank you for the trust you've placed in me. As your Co-Presidents, Pedro and I will work tirelessly to build this city..." Her words were barely audible over the roar of the crowd.

In Our Bones

Remembrance

Ben's knees creaked as he stood up from his nap and grabbed the worn wood cane that was propped next to his bed. He shuffled out into the main room where the rest of the family had gathered. As soon as he emerged, the kids shouted, "Grandpa! We've been waiting for you!"

"Sorry. It takes me a little longer to get going these days." His skin was creviced and his voice dry, but his eyes were bright as ever.

Ben's granddaughter Elena said with feigned impatience, "Well, it's almost time to start the party. Aunt Dj and Uncle Li are on their way." Elena shouted into the kitchen, "Grandma! Grampa's up."

Petra's pink-beaded necklace and matching skirt swayed as she shuffled into the room and side squeezed Ben. She searched his face to see if he was well, as old wives tend to do with their husbands. Petra didn't call him Ben anymore, though. No one did. It was either Dad, Grandpa or Emilio. Though of course Petra also had her pet names.

243

Emilio, Petra, and their adult children had moved to Nacia about ten years before. Medeina had been completed under Lauren and Pedro's time in office. It was a glorious city, but never had the bells, whistles, and life support systems of Nacia. Since birth rates never kept up with deaths, in time Nacia's population decreased. A lottery was set up to allow residents of Medeina to move over to Nacia as space allowed. Khadija had moved to Nacia a few years previously, and the whole family had been reunited in one city again.

Even before they moved, though, the resources of Nacia were available to use, and Emilio worked with a librarian there to track down his history. After weeks of combing, he came across photos of a young woman with eyes like huge pools of sorrow that he feared could drown him. It was the same woman in the crumpled black and white picture the social worker pressed into Rachel's hands all those years before. Her name was Clair and her social media posts showed someone who had revealed her pain for all the world for all to see and no one to care. She named her son Emilio, which was the name that Ben chose for himself from then on. He printed out several of the happier photos of Clair and added them to his dresser along with the photo strip of the two of them together. Emilio's life story was finally complete, or at least as near as it would ever be. A frozen spot in his heart thawed, and some of the anger he'd scarcely known he carried faded away.

At the party, Petra kissed Emilio on the cheek. "Mi amor," she murmured.

A child sitting nearby sniggered. Emilio grabbed her hand and kissed it back. Their eight-year-old grandson brought them in small pieces of fluffy white cake with red sprinkles on top, and a small girl delivered cold cups of wild ginger punch. Petra and Emilio snuggled together on the couch. Their marriage had had its difficulties, but more ups than downs. When they'd gone through a rough patch early on, not long after their oldest was born, their friends and family helped them work it out. They stayed together and raised three children – two boys and a girl. Seven grandchildren followed.

Parties and rites of passage were an important part of life in Nacia and Medeina. Different families had their own traditions that sometimes others joined, but Ruby and James had wanted to create a holiday that could bring everyone together. So, they designated two weeks each year when residents took off from non-essential work. Chores that had to be done were split up as much as possible so that no one had to keep on the job while others took leisure. James wanted everyone to stay grounded, though. So, he suggested a Remembrance Day smack dab in the middle of the festivities to honor those they'd lost and to keep in mind lessons learned. The holiday was designated by a certain phase of the moon, at a certain time of the year. This night was not the night of parties and dancing, but of quiet enchantment – candles and incense, flowers, and soft music. Nacia and Medeina's children would complain of the boredom only to grow into adults who cherished the holiday, as it goes with life.

Khadija at a certain point in her own life realized that her parent's religion was not her own. She removed her hijab and took the name Dija. She and her partner Li never married but were together all the same. They shimmered into the party wearing their coordinating jewel-tone clothing with gold accents, her gray hair in a short cut. Dija was quick on her feet and sharp witted. When Dija came into the gathering, she exclaimed, "Happy Remembrance Day" to everyone and no one at the same time. The party gleefully shouted it back. Some of the children came over and gave them hugs. Dija and Li were raising their shy granddaughter, Calla, since her parents died in an accident. Calla slunk in, all arms and legs, behind Papa Li. Calla's friend grabbed her and the two of them scattered into the crowd.

Remembrance Day was typically kicked off by the eldest member of whatever clan of family and friends had assembled that day. For their bunch, the job fell to Dija. After she finished, Emilio pushed his way up off the soft couch and gave her a long embrace. He whispered in her ear, "I love you, sister" then waddled over to the center of the room. He liked to keep his speeches lighter than some. He started, "Dija, those were beautiful words. I'm afraid that I don't have anything so thoughtful to follow. But I do have some stories for you. Are you ready to hear them?" The kids clapped loudly. Emilio and several other family members were the oral historians of their clan. Ruby encouraged people to adopt this ancient tradition to keep the mind fresh and stories near. Emilio had taken it on with gusto.

For his speech, he waded back to his grandmother Ann's parents and told what he knew about their lives. Then he proceeded through the generations. Emilio added in some chronicles of his birth mom, as he'd been able to piece together, too. But the stories that really excited him were of the good years after they moved to Medeina.

Lauren and Erik lived blessed and full lives to the end. She was co-president for their full six-year term, and both she and Pedro were beloved. After, Lauren went back to her first love of gardening and stayed mostly out of public life. She was a warm and dedicated grandmother to Emilio's children and died quietly in her seventies surrounded by those who loved her.

Emilio had difficulty standing for long and had about reached his limit regaling the children with fun memories. "I've got one last thought for you. I know, you're disappointed. 'Grandpa, please go on,' I think I hear you saying?"

The children yelled "NO!" realizing that he was pulling their legs.

Emilio chuckled. "This last part is a little more for the adults in the bunch. My adoptive mom, Rachel, died when I was still so young. Oh, how I miss her even now. But I still remember how she always used to say that she wanted me to be somewhere safe, somewhere I could grow old. My hips were really bothering me the other day, and I realized, I'm not young."

Someone called out playfully, "You're right, you're old!" Emilio and everyone laughed.

As they quieted down, his tone grew somber. Emilio studied the faces of his kids, grandkids, and his closest friends and was filled with wonder. He thought back on his life and the trials, tribulations and instances of unbounded kindness and strange circumstance that had brought him to this stitch in time. Dija caught his gaze and tears unexpectedly streamed from his eyes. Grief, love, joy, and hope intertwined into an indistinguishable singular mix.

"It was Rachel's vision that brought us here. With the state of the world being what it is and the Wars of the Cross raging still in the United States, I don't know what would have become of me otherwise. We went through a lot of scary times before we got here. But we overcame it all, together. So, yes, my mom died trying to get me here, and then my Aunt Lauren made sure she got me and Dija the rest of the way. Lauren was really busy when we got here, so Dija and I kind of raised ourselves after that with some help from our Uncle Erik. But Lauren did her best and she loved us with all she had, and I know it wasn't easy for her. It wasn't easy for my mom, either. So, today I want to give a toast in their honor."

He raised his cup.

"To you, Mom and Lauren. You are forever loved and will forever be missed. You did your job well because I am undeniably, unquestionably, completely… an old man. Now, go! Have some fun!"

The children bounced up and out in a flash, giggling as they fell over each other to get to the games ahead.

Epilogue

Insects chirped in the shadowy verdant fields, and the stars shone bright as ever. The walls shielding Nacia were crumbling and dainty flowers and herbs peeked about in its jagged crevices. This perimeter of stone and clay had been a silent witness to Earth's utter annihilation and bit-by-bit revival. Moonlight rippled across the surface of the lake as two boys, almost men, laid in the poking stubbles of grass along the bank. They dreamed tumultuous dreams of trekking the planet and exploring the ruins of a vanished civilization. The boys longed to visit the other settlements where humanity had clung to survival and return to Nacia with a hero's welcome.

Outside the city, the boys felt wild and renewed. Their senses were sharper. They took in the breeze flowing across their skin and the light rustle of grass. Embedded in their psyche was the story of what had happened to the world, and the boys felt fortunate to be on the other side of the madness. Yet the Earth was a different place than it had been when the high walls of Nacia were built.

Raging fires, leveling storms, rising seas and mass extinctions had all taken their toll.

The boys' Earth was filled by handfuls of plants, animals and other life that were tough enough to endure. The others, spellbinding and majestic, had been lost to time. Like a cruel joke of chemistry, acid-laden hot oceans turned a brilliant shade of blue and their waters billowed with ghostly jellyfish.

Over centuries the miasma cleared, and the climate stabilized. And life strived to live. Successive layers of creation grew one on top of the other. Spores of rebirth. All the tenacious beings that weathered the storm speciated, and over the course of several million years filled the planet once again with biological wonder.

Gaia was not in a hurry. She had seen epochs of life come and go before. Still and all, the Anthropocene era was over.

Acknowledgements

Writing this novel took more out of me than I could have ever realized when I began. As such, it took a lot out of my whole family. I am eternally grateful for their support during such a grueling process. They understood why I believed this was so important and were my biggest fans. My son Jacob provided moral support and encouragement and listened to me vent when needed. My daughter Jessica would bring me food and coffee when I was too busy to eat. My daughter Maria was an absolute rock star throughout - helping with her little brothers, bringing me endless cups of coffee and rarely complaining about any of it. My son Justin helped me work through sticky plot points and was kind and gentle when I was overwhelmed with it all. James let me use his name for one of my main characters, gave me wonderful hugs and kisses whenever I needed them, and was endlessly patient with my continual distraction. It is for you all that I wrote this novel, because I want you all to have the chance to grow old in peace and safety. You've made this highly imperfect woman a much better one by being your mom. I love you always.

Lois Kennis gave numerous important suggestions throughout that helped me define and improve the project. Maggiy Emery took time out of her busy schedule to answer any question I had about the literary process, read drafts and made suggestions that undoubtedly led to a better end product. Michelle Pohl Guilfoil provided great suggestions and encouragement. Hahn Chang read early chapters and provided insights into perspective and character that were invaluable. Alice Deshelia Blackmon went through a pivotal chapter for me at a time when I was freaking out and helped assure me that I was on the right track. I so much appreciate it. Tami Greenslade contributed detailed clear edits that made the novel stronger. Before I had any idea at all what I was doing, Becky Barrette helped me see that it was possible. Fred Iutzi spent hours on the phone with me talking through any esoteric question I had and letting me swear and vent when I needed.

There are many specific teachers who I want to thank, but I wanted to take a moment to thank teachers in general. You work harder and longer each day for less pay and acknowledgement than you deserve. If it weren't for the compassion of so many great teachers over the years, I would likely have been lost. There are a few teachers and professors of mine who had a particularly big impact that I want to acknowledge by name. In high school, Kay Schwarz taught rhetoric and was tough as nails, but that woman kicked my butt into shape and made me a writer. Peter Heimer was my literature teacher, and the first to recognize talent in me. He sent me to a young writer's workshop that provided a glimpse into a world of ideas and intellectualism that would become extremely important to me. At Scott Community College, Mark Aronson was a tireless advocate for his students and the world. He taught me some of the most important concepts that underlie this novel. Thank you. Finally, I would be remiss if I didn't point to my dear friend, Ricardo Salvador. Ricardo was an amazing teacher, friend, boss and mentor whose belief in me was instrumental to my becoming the person I am. I can never thank him enough for everything.

Another blanket acknowledgement I want to make is for the journalists, writers and others who are doing the grueling and sometimes dangerous work each day to keep the world informed and hold the powerful to account. I began listening to National Public Radio on my early morning commute to work nearly thirty years ago, and it kept my mind active during the many years as a stay-home mom. A while back I discovered podcasts and those became my go-to for news and information. I want to point to several that were highly influential in creating this novel or helped keep me entertained while writing it. These podcasts include Bundyville: The Remnant, It Could Happen Here, Hot Take, Drilled, The Women's War, Throughline, Trump, Inc., Groundtruth, Up First, Today Explained, The Daily, Family Secrets, and Carrier.

Last, though by no means least, I want to thank Cherie Macenka, Sian Hyleg, Liz Hurst and everyone at Between the Lines Publishing. You saw potential in a rough manuscript and stuck with me through my fear, anxiety and sometimes panic about this project. You were patient and helped make a stressful project a little less so. I owe you more gratitude than words can express.

Pernell Plath Meier

Pernell Plath Meier grew up on the Iowa side of the Mississippi in the Quad Cities. She left behind a life of traumatic chaos to move out on her own at fifteen. She earned undergraduate science degrees with honors in biology, anthropology, and environmental studies, followed by graduate degrees in sustainable agriculture and anthropology at Iowa State University. She's worked and traveled in ten countries, including a long-ago trip to see the Grateful Dead in Canada. After college, she moved to Kentucky to help farmers transition from tobacco production to local foods. She found her way to Southeast Minnesota and spent nearly twenty years raising gardens, chickens, dogs and cats, while homeschooling her five adopted children. Today Pernell juggles day to day life as a single mom with three kids still at home, a smaller flock of chickens and a new puppy, Buddy. Prior writings have centered on adoption and gardening. In Our Bones is her first quest as a novelist.